NIGHT TRAIN

Night Train

STORIES

LISE ERDRICH

COFFEE HOUSE PRESS
MINNEAPOLIS

Coffee House Press books are available to the trade through our primary distributor, Consortium Book Sales & Distribution, www.cbsd.com or (800) 283-3572. For personal orders, catalogs, or other information, write to: Coffee House Press, 27 North Fourth Street, Suite 400, Minneapolis, MN 55401.

Coffee House Press is a nonprofit literary publishing house. Support from private foundations, corporate giving programs, government programs, and generous individuals helps make the publication of our books possible. We gratefully acknowledge their support in detail in the back of this book.

Good books are brewing at coffeehousepress.org

LIBRARY OF CONGRESS CATALOGING-IN-PUBLICATION DATA
Erdrich, Liselotte.
Night train : stories / by Lise Erdrich.
p. cm.
ISBN-13: 978-1-56689-202-5 (alk. paper)
ISBN-10: 1-56689-202-3 (alk. paper)
[1. Indians of North America—Fiction.] 1. Title.
PS3605.R37N54 2008
813'.6—DC22
2007017786
FIRST EDITION | FIRST PRINTING
1 3 5 7 9 8 6 4 2
Printed in the United States

This work was created with the support of a 1989 John Hove creative writing fellowship from the North Dakota Council on the Arts. The author wishes to express her sincere gratitude and appreciation.

Versions of these stories first appeared in the following journals: "Beehive" in *Many Mountains Moving;* "Dirty Rice" in *Newport Review;* "Door" in *Clockwatch Review;* "Great Love Poems of the State Hospital in *XCP: Cross Cultural Poetics;* "Jolly Beef, Métis Legend" in *North Dakota Quarterly;* "Other (Explain)" in *Paragraph;* "Still Life with 'Marigolds' & The Blue Mumbled Earth" in *Cream City Review;* "Tribe Unknown (Fleur-de-Lis)" in *Sister Nations: Native American Writers on Community* (Minnesota Historical Society Press); "XXXL" in *Minnesota Monthly;* "Wi-Jun-Jon" in *Four Directions;* "Zanimoo" in *South Dakota Review* and *Aboriginal Voices;* "Hairy Buffalo," "Night Train," and "ERRR" in *Traffic.* "Night Train" also appeared in *Yellow Medicine Review.*

NIGHT TRAIN

CONTENTS

Author lost the keys again, author shuffles through piles of paper on the desk where they might be hiding, shuffles through overstuffed drawers, sees a few ideas in there, digs in pockets and finds the keys and more ideas again, but the phone rings and time gets away again so author hurryup gets in the car and on the highway and many miles toward a specific destination with random ideas chasing far ahead of her, tuned into classic rock radio ("'Scuse me, while I kiss the sky!"), scanning ahead and to the sides for birds and animals or whatever there is to see out there and then while checking the makeup job in the rearview, 2000 Calorie Mascara, Berry Nice Lipstick! sees the flashing lights again, but quickly seeking cracks in the delay spots a name tag on the officer's pocket and a family resemblance to someone whose story she can tell so the officer sheepishly gives her a warning instead of ticket, author gets away one more time but shows up late as usual, reads the papers to the audience and the pages are somehow out of order but nobody knows the difference so the author clips along to the ending and almost gets away clean, except for Q & A: a person raises their hand and asks "How do you think of these things?" and the author explodes in loud delight, laughing "Good god how do you *not* think of these things?" and sees a sudden brick wall of puzzled eyes zooming straight ahead and all the atoms that were happily spinning overhead could now be the world spinning away beneath her feet but not to lose one's footing, the author dances offstage with Looney Tunes music, that's all folks! and in the long run it won't matter since they're just a crowd of strangers and the curtains yank shut on all this at the road sign *Baskin-Robbins Ice Cream 31 Flavors Next Exit.*

AUTUMN

One of the times that Z came back from college, everyone was over at the neighbor's house eating a turkey and having a party to celebrate the colors. They were two families quite used to this sort of thing. The turkey was a gigantic gleaming brown fellow surrounded by candied violets, crystal dishes of jellied cranberries, and such. Mrs. Abercrombie felt the need to decorate with a harvest theme. Rather, she required an occasion—the silk maple leaf festoonery, clever pumpkins, mosaic corn, cornucopian trip. Mr. Abercrombie was a grandfather clock ticking in the foyer. Z's brothers ran in and out of the place laughing joking, and wrestled on the lawn.

There was a pointy old fence of black iron spears around it, unusual. It was an overdone 1890s house in a 1901 neighborhood in a maple tree section of the state capital in the 1970s. At this time of year, a hundred years ago, at the top of a furry brown hill, alone. The trees were not yet planted. An ostentatious landmark, the new Victorian with its towers watching a town grow out of prairie. Under the bluest blue sky the wheat was goldly waving, the threshers kept steaming, a line of comely draft horses twitched their curvely muscles and, waiting, sighed . . . the days were made of apple-cider light and grain dust. Houses climbed up the hill and sat down around their neighbors, dressed up in early-1900s fashions. Kitty-corner, the wooden ex-governor's mansion yet stands, in a handsome new coat of charcoal gray with black trim. People would go down the sidewalks, kicking up bright maple, oak leaves thinking, Oh, what a perfect picture, because—

Trick or treat! It is Halloween! And then if any turkey holidays came along there'd be lovely snow, how nice to come in from: The ceremonial brisk yard-rakings, sidewalk-shovelings, strolls.

Mr. Abercrombie, a lifelong friend of the family, had died years ago leaving the Mrs. to fuss about with her arts and crafts. Every so often the canny old bird sprang *kook*ing out of the clockwork causing her to address him by name with various rambling remarks and reports. At a certain time he'd remind the household to sit down and eat their oatmeal and so on. Somehow, Z understood that Abercrombie made a final bargain of Z's mother and father to look after his Mrs. because she was arrrr, somewhat off, a wee bit. There were the sons to raise and then they were gone, grown, successful, didn't come back too often. There was still the eldest daughter Z looked up to like a sister, a pacific maiden with long sorrowful dark hair, the occasional flute or dulcimer. Drooping medieval costumes of the 1970s were draped on her affectedly as she curled up in the bartizan with a basket of embroidery, book of poetry, strings of beads and wild feathers: ring-neck pheasant, green-wing teal, vermilion-shafted flicker. It was all some sort of performance art or fetish, Z decided, recalling a childhood in which she had been overcome with specialness to be given a birthday neck-lace—*how awfully nice to be remembered!*—from the very hands of such a creature. Melodious lark, ferruginous hawk! Chuck-will's-widow, prairie falcon, pipit.

Then there was the daughter to whom the occasion was verbally pledged, a toast then! as her betrothal had just been announced. Never had the blackbird nuns of the school they had attended together, Z and this younger daughter, ever let on that there was anything amiss about the latter. They were souls, you see. All was calm, all was bright, every morning they walked together to the strict brick turn-of-the-century schoolhouse and their guardian angels waited in the creaky dark wood-worked hallway until it was time to hover over the mon-key bars or crosswalk, go home. Thursday mornings, a stained-glass cathedral where the holy thundering organ and narcotic Latin habituated Z to prayer. It was not until years later that Z understood her fellow soul to be what they called retarded. Very Special. Or some acronym these days, like as not still inapt. In any case, the younger daughter was blue-eyed blond, bland and good and would always, always be good, a pure soul. There was nothing wrong in her face and that is the only thing Z ever noticed—Z would never see her expression as dull, but almost anyone else might.

Mrs. Abercrombie had china in an acorn-and-oak leaf-pattern, also folding trays from the dawn of TV dinners in that same trend. Z's mother had a couch like that once, maybe curtains. They were two women who lingered in the 1950s. That fiancée guy kept passing choice dishes to Z in a solicitous and patriarchal way. Z had a vague impression of Li'l Abner or Jethro Bodine. Mind you, not his speech or clothes or manners or anything like that you could see; who knows what it was. Not his face. Z was seventeen. Dreamy-giggling in a slight rose-gold haze of marijuana smoke lately, teasing the little brothers and displeasing others, Z just wanted to play as before in their years at the Holy Ghost School. Why was this man marrying the poor girl when even Z, who could if she wanted to, didn't want to grow up? He must be so old, in his thirties. What a hick thing to do, so perverted, or was it inverted? Like people who married their cousins and kin.

It should be a sin. Z looked at the grown-ups to see how they really felt about it, but Mrs. Abercrombie had joined a new religion. (This caused her to smile beatifically at all times at all things.) Naturally the younger daughter would follow it too, this is how she could end up with a husband. And him, some sort of deacon. A probable zealot looking to gain a house and servant; but then again, maybe he saw something beautiful in his child bride. With a sudden startle Z realized she had glimpsed the eldest daughter in the turret with her zither playing and singing "Scarborough Fair" and also knitting a baby bootie. The thought of the little unformed bootie struck Z with terror. She exploded from the table unexcused, causing little concentric waves of *Oh my goodness!* and *Wha?* and *Hmmmmm*, dashed out the door down the steps, diving into a pile of leaves rolling around and around screaming, barking, wrestling with Sparkplug her dear pudgy bulldog.

Sparky, Oh Sparky! I love you little puppy, why can't we live forever, Z said to the grizzled, arthritic old beast. Evening shadows reached across the tawny lawn, boldly shuffled the brilliant gold coins tottering on a row of poplars. The shadows advanced in long cool fingers, reaching up into the leaves, slyly husbanding a hoard, then felt their way smoothly over the walnut and maple and mahogany indoors. They played with the lace doilies and heirlooms and photogravures, the Indian-corn accents, as they slid into the dining room and parlor and scattered everyone away. Off to the movie-show, football game, sister's date! Of course the younger sister vowed to stay home and wash dishes, clean up. Z was happy to join her since they could sing loud stupid songs together while they splashed suds and danced and they could burn leaves and marshmallows outside after that. Bonfires were a fondest memory of Z. The brothers and sisters would rake the conjoined lawn into a great leaf bank and play in it until dark when the mothers and fathers came out and oversaw the torching, wienie roast, singsong. The eldest sister invented ghost stories, games she called Salem Witch Trials, Powhatan's Powwow, Go See. By firelight and a possible sliver of moon, the orange-and-black adult faces recalled to Z in her mind's eye like famous rock features or totem poles on some old tourist highway postcard, solid and eternal. Z thought they'd do this one more time and then she'd go back to college and disappear into the future just like she was supposed to.

Shrieking with mirth, Z and the younger sister threw armfuls of bright bits at one another, took turns being buried under luminous expired biological shapes. A kindly old tire swing hung from the huge ancient cottonwood that rained down gold upon the scene. From the shriveling garden the two friends gathered a final bouquet. The younger sister eulogized Z, concluding "She was so beautiful that no one would tell her, so she lived all her life being shy." Deeply embarrassed, Z wiggled out of the leaves saying she had to use the bathroom, and bounded into the house. It is true, Z was thinking, there is something wrong with me, why can't I be like all the cheerleaders and sluts. Z was going to go look in the mirrors upstairs, trying out different fearless smiles and radiant faces and sexual poses she didn't dare show a single solitary other human being. The mirrors upstairs were grand, very many in the bedrooms and bathrooms. Z loved the full-length one with a rich mahogany frame, curved like a courtesan, in the guest bedroom, protected from view by heavy wine-velvet gold-tasseled drapes.

It was a room of shadows cast from ornate and narcissistic museum-quality antiques: tall dark wardrobe, chiffonier, chifforobe. Walnut dresser, birds-eye bureau, armoire. Like a moth, Z was drawn to the adjoining bathroom with 1920s electric candles that caused everything inside it to be bathed in warm golden light, even the cold white porcelain claw-foot tub, frost-glass mirrors, and Z. Every fixture shone yellow.

Z paused at the foot of the stairs. There was the clock, but not the tick. Z listened. The house was large and quiet with so much dark woodwork and so many rooms. Z had never given the fiancée another thought; at the dining table barely glanced at his face, since it might look like some type of raptor. But now she felt his presence. She had ignored his gaze at dinner. What was he? other than a big stealthy body with no face that she should recognize. Z ascended the stairs already enjoying herself as a nude portrait in the dark mirror, something glowing white and weightless, though she could step right into the gold-lit bathroom and see: someone shiny, like a diamond! an hourglass! a peach! with lovely-long-curly-gold-red-chestnut hair, an ivory complexion, and rose-petal cheeks! A red-apple mouth, perfect teeth! Look at me! Of the seven deadly sins Z believed she had just Vanity, which she could keep hidden from all humans and view in secret only now and then.

Z pulled off her sweatshirt, stepped out of her jeans at the top of the stairs. Seven steps more and her hand was on the doorknob, Z moved through the dim bedroom to turn to the bathroom, when the bedroom door flung shut behind her. Something made her look in the long curving mirror where her glowing-white body always stood. Z stopped and jumped the same moment she glanced in a sinistral direction. It was not her pale unclothed shape in the mirror. It was him. Oh, excuse me, Z said quite shaken. So sorry, I was looking for the bathroom. She could have found it with her eyes closed: her hand reaching surely to the light switch that many times before this. Z turned toward the bedroom door again but after four steps her feet were tangled in bed sheets, mired in glue, stuck. Z could not move. She stood there for a century, not looking. Why you are buck naked Z bravely said. Then his hands were on her shoulders.

The hands were strangely heavy, invested with some dense supernormal energy that descended like a judgment, commanding the mortal body by touch, the mind a dumb numbness that watched from afar what transpired, what the two bodies did, which was . . . terrible, unstoppable, absolute, and in a searing pulse of amazed intuition Z perceived that this cruel and greedy-swift power was coming from . . . Z. The hands were on her exactly, turning her admiringly, like a precious priceless vase with the perfect words spelled in Z's very own mind. He was behind her, Z felt his strength against her, his glowing form pressed to hers. Z in the mirror saw one anima overtake another in the weird familiar dark. With his sudden profusion of flattering lingual maneuvers Z squeezed her eyes shut, saw sparklings, a luminous amoeba of stars engulfing black velvet. He was bending her over the massive old four-poster bed, both of them kneeling so that he was whispering obscene prayers to Z, to her hair. His face buried in it groaning, though Z could only wonder why he'd feel pain and only said once, shyly mumbling, I never did this before and he breathed into her hair I know and the other thing she said trembling was Why are you doing this. Because I love you he confessed in her hair and Z was satisfied, even though: her whole being went off just like that, imploding, exploding as he strove in vain. Z was about to say something urgent but he was already shuddering against her and with an odd wounded cry he was gone, and then Z heard a cold formal male voice tell her "Good-bye" and she answered as stiffly, "I see."

She didn't even give him another look. Pulled on her clothes, skipped down the stairs, never did see his face. Z would not forget those omniscient hands with their precise philology, how that big-hick dick would say such words to her when he was such a strapping figurehead and deacon. She made him do it, wished the pleasuring words onto his tongue. It was her own vain volition that committed the transgression, just so she could exact her own selfish deviant variant of oral gratification: his intricate involuntary lingual maneuvers had somehow freed her. But, thought Z, technically nothing happened—he has not been unfaithful, nor have I to the husband I someday will have. Once in a while, though, Z would wake up next to her wedded husband and realize that something had made her experience a perfectly perfect ! in her dreams. She knew what. The words. When Z hopped out the kitchen door and across the yard to the leaf pile, she found the fair bride-to-be stretched out very still and pale on her mound. From the clasp of her hands a flurry of withered petals had scattered all about her. Z looked for a long time at the flawless sleeping cream-of-wheat face. A tear slid out of Z's eye like a diamond. She was a perfect angel, Z said and ran away.

It was a honeymoon with a man driving a new pickup truck with his beautiful new bride beside him and a new RV trailing them across the flat hot desert. The bride really was very new, in fact just legally an adult who had co-signed all the loans in the same happily trusting way she did anything with this man. After all, he was so handsome.

The immense and jagged mountain ranges rose up all around this tiny movement in the vast and arid scene. There was no other traffic on the highway, not even a grazing herd of anything on the slopes.

"Look! A gas station/restaurant," cried the bride. "We better stop because who knows when we'll get another chance." The building was a low-slung inconspicuous rectangle of weathered gray lumber without the normal tall soaring name-brand petroleum sign that could light up the night or be seen from any distance.

They went inside and sat down. The waitress had a high teased burnt-orange hairdo. "That's why it's called the Beehive State," the bride whispered, but her husband needed the joke explained. The bride felt suddenly cold. She felt this in the pit of her stomach, without even taking a sip of her ice water, which she had raised to her lips but set back down on the red-and-white checkered tablecloth.

It was not the first time she had noticed something missing in his mind. This realization, combined with the matching pattern of the table and curtains, caused her to shake violently. He ignored this and studied the menu as if it contained more significant clues. She gripped her knees to still herself. Her thoughts buzzed in panic. The waitress wore a turquoise pantsuit with the same color eyeshadow. The waitress had a face that matched the dry landscape: orange and brown powder makeup, deep cracks and lines, and rouged hollow cheeks. The waitress had burnt-orange lipstick and nail polish. This was no place to live. What if this waitress were only twenty-five or thirty years old? Or else an alien being.

The bride wanted to leave right this instant. She could warn her husband about the food. She knew that every item on the menu would be a frozen formed oval with a different color food-service sauce to approximate its description, e.g., Veal Parmigiana, Chicken-Fried Steak with Cream Gravy, Salisbury Steak, Chicken Marinara. In the kitchen there'd be gallon plastic containers of red, brown, orange, and white multipurpose supreme sauce. She had served her waitress time at the Summer Shack on school vacations.

But it was she who had wanted to stop here. Nor could she bear to invite that blank, defective stare. His high school yearbook had many girls with beehive hair-dos. He lived with his mother between marriages until he was thirty-one. The house was kept "immaculate," some-one had remarked. His mother had given her a cookbook with a red-and-white checkered cover as a wedding gift. It was presented with a lengthy verbal explanation of how to correctly hard-cook an egg since those instructions were not included in the cookbook. It was a very disturb-ing experience, but she patiently accepted this informa-tion since it had seemed so important to her husband's mother. Soon she was trapped and frightened by a con-stant swarm of detailed household hints, even if she answered the phone.

The menu was a laminated sheet listing the dinner menu on one side (each served with a choice of potato and soup or salad). He was eating the Salisbury Steak with mashed potatoes and a wedge of iceberg lettuce with orange dressing, but it could have been anything else on the suddenly-doomed planet. "I love you, you're so pretty," he stated. She wasn't looking at him, though, since he sounded like a robot and she was looking out the window thinking about what would never happen, even if she jumped up right then and ran into the desert screaming and crying and naked. Outer space had been described to her in grade school as a cold and empty vac-uum where humans could not breathe.

CORN IS NUMBER ONE

The earth was built on the back of a Turtle after the Flood, as everybody knows. Sky Woman fell to earth just as all the birds and animals had finished the job. When she landed, she gave birth to a daughter. This daughter became a young woman and one day she was pregnant. "Who did that?" Sky Woman asked. "It was the West Wind," her daughter replied. She gave birth to twin boys and died. These boys ran off in order to cause various stories all over the earth.

For a moment, you may call them G. Howdy and G.I. Joe. Sky Woman told them, "You will have four sisters to mind you when I'm gone." Sky Woman buried her daughter and sang a sacred song over the dirt. Corn, then Squash and Bean grew out of the ground right there. Sky Woman sent these spirits of the garden to find People. They were inside of seeds, carried on the wind, and by the birds and animals. Old Magic Woman found them.

Old Magic Woman was always digging around. She would look at things and think of what to call them. She decided to invent Native American Agriculture. She made a clearing among the cottonwood trees down by the river, she worked the soil with her digging stick. The buck deer came out of the trees and raked the ground with their horns. Later, the deer came back to rake weeds. They came back one more time to eat, and they shed their horns. Old Magic Woman tied the horns onto a stick to make her own garden rake. The people followed what Old Magic Woman did, and they prospered.

Old Magic Woman went out to gather firewood. When she came back she said, "I saw the gooseberry leaves open up today, so it is time to plant the seeds that Raven brought to us." She made a hill of dirt and buried the seeds, and gave them plenty of water.

Along came the oldest sister, Corn. At first she was like a small shoot of grass. The girls and the women and birds sang to Corn to make it grow tall and straight and strong. "They sing my praises," thought Corn. "The sky is the limit, so I shall not quit." Even when Corn had grown quite high and sturdy, the girls and women kept watch over her and chased away all the birds and animals and boys who might be hungry. "When the geese come back it is time to plant the Corn again," they sang. "When the boys come to smile at us we will send them on their way."

Corn thought, "I am the single most important plant in America." This was true: everything in America and eventually the whole planet would somehow involve Corn. For those who need independent verification, simply Google "the importance of corn." With the quotation marks removed there will be at least 1,250,000 internet entries. However, if you insist on typing "Corn is Number One," you may only find one entry, in which Corn is implicated in the case of a constipated dog who is discussed in a veterinary forum.

Meanwhile, Corn looked down and saw something interesting. A tubular thing came out of the ground and unfolded its green wings. But instead of flying away, it sent out a long green feeler and started to climb onto Corn.

"What are you doing! You're going to strangle me, get off! Can't you stand on your own!" cried the Corn.

"No," said the Bean, "This is what I do." It continued to make its way up by wrapping itself around and around, hugging onto Corn. "And furthermore, it is for your own good that you support me. I can do lots of good tricks. I can take the air and turn it into nitrogen for your roots. I can turn you into a complete protein. I can make you famous: there will be a song called "Beans and Cornbread" on TV. Yeah, you need me. I have more surprises after this," said Bean.

Corn was not a hugger, but that was the situation.

Then along came Squash. Two blunt shiny green sprouts split into more and more leaves, and the leaves grew huge and floppy on long prickly vines. Squash spread out all over like a blanket or shawl around the Corn and Bean plants. Broad and humble and ground-hugging and patient and lying low was the Squash.

"Is that all you do?" asked the Bean. Squash said, "Look, I have both male and female blossoms," and two gigantic yellow flowers burst open, shocking Corn and

Bean. They shut up. "And my leaves will keep the ground moist and shady and weed free, so your roots will not dry up in the heat of the Sun, while my itchy vines will discourage the hungry animals, and there are big colorful fruits hiding underneath these leaves."

The spirit of Corn, being a creative and adventurous risk-taker, began to feel stifled with this arrangement, always under wraps. Corn wandered off in the cool of the night, wanting to find and collect the dews that came to the earth on moonbeams. Corn thought, "I am sure that I have magic powers to attract the night mist and fog that drip from my leaves in the morning, which my sisters are always drinking, although it is I who make this happen."

As soon as Corn left, a being known as Chi-Jyawb came and blighted the garden. The spirits of Bean and Squash were crushed beneath its dark moldy disposition. Chi-Jyawb went after Corn and took her captive in his abode deep beneath the surface of the earth. Corn wept. She wept and sang a germinal song to feel her way out of this mess.

A little animal was listening to the gentle breeze, which picked up the lament from a hole in the ground. The little animal did not immediately comprehend the Corn language, but being moved by the strange silky voice, formulated a response using the highly evolved, complex, sophisticated, yet divinely-designed vocabulary of a prairie dog.

Thus alarmed, Sun sent a messenger in search of Corn because of the germinating tune that lingered in the air.

The messenger called to Corn and, shining a light into the black tunnel of Chi-Jyawb, led her back to the garden where her sisters were dying of thirst.

Corn made a promise to the Sun that she would never again leave the garden until the harvest time was over and all the seeds were safely stored away. The Sun stationed its messenger to keep watch over the garden from that day forward.

"Who are you, and why are you beaming at us like that?" asked Corn, Squash, and Bean when they saw the stranger.

"I am your new sister the Sunflower, and it is my job to project a positive mental attitude. I will stand to the north, and thus encourage all living things in this beautiful and scientifically sound ecosystem, which is our joint accomplishment."

The pressure was off, because Sunflower could stand with Corn, which would take the heat off Bean and Squash, who could just go and do their things now. So then Sunflower called forth the little animal whose voice she had heard, and gave to her a beautiful green shawl with corn-silk tassels and intertwined designs of leaves and vines and flowers that was spontaneously generated from a song, which got all messed up in translation but went something like this:

Mandidoominens, Little Spirit Seeds. I am but one in the design. Of the scroll, of the spiraling vine, flowering tendrils of the scarlet runner a red spark I glimpsed like hope, like the sweet wild strawberry oday-imin on a spear of light in the shade of a forest that signified our origins.

Oday, the poor heart of a human being. Send us light, the "little spirit seeds" are in your hands, dear holy curvilinear path flowering through all time and trespass, five fingers of the hawthorn leaf like a hand to hold this crown of mysteries.

Lead us from all darkness, bead by bead by bead. As it was in the beginning is now and ever shall be, as it is manifest in this greenery this vinery this leafery, the fingers work in your own language: I believe in the Almighty, Creator of heaven and earth; And I believe each and every deed is a bead, is a seed, is a need, is in every one of us, unfurling the vine, still growing.

W ell O.K., you take a pound and a half of ground beef and fry it up in oil with chopped onions and a cup and a half of rice, just raw, uncooked long grain white rice, and if you want Wild & Dirty Rice you might want to parboil the wild rice first before you add it to the fryins and cut the white in half. Shake on a whole lot of Louisiana powder while you're fryin and grind some good black pepper onto it at some point and do not forget the Tabasco. If you have some garden peppers chop them up and throw them in, and if you want Drunk & Dirty Rice then crack a beer or two or three meanwhile and throw some on the fryins when it's all browned and then put on the cover, you could use just water I suppose but I never do. And if you want Dirty Bloody Rice just throw in the Snap-E-Tom or a can of stewed tomatoes or tomato juice if you got some. You could use chicken livers like the bona fide but myself I do not want to think about my own liver let alone what has happened to a chicken. It just isn't right. Drunk & Dirty & Bloody Rice is about my speed today and it'll fix you up good, watch this! "The crowd roars its approval" when we introduce old Snap-E-Tom and Buddy Weiser. Yep I get a thunderous standin ovation for my cookin show. Never mind about the beans because rice and beans is just a whole nother subject and that's enough for now.

A man arrived at the threshold. Looking out, he saw his wife. She faced the car in the driveway, wrestling from it their children and bags of groceries. Tender feelings paid a visit. He opened the door, and with his rough, competent hands he grasped the catch and slid on the ring that would hold it and make it secure. Then he went to help her.

They passed one another in the driveway. The beautiful laughing children skipped and tangled about them, their voices bright butterfly wings. The man took some of the load and his wife the rest and last. He went straight to the kitchen without a look back. He could hear the happy butterflies lilting along in the breezeway, alighting here, there—and safely indoors. He began to put the groceries away. He was a methodical man who liked to have things in their place.

The rip and crunch of metal froze him.

He should have known. It was exactly like her to do such a clumsy pigheaded thing; she had no respect for things mechanical, no regard for practical workings, no comprehension of hydraulics or shear, not a functional thought in her brain: only foolish high-flying liberal-arts-academia dreams. He was a working man and master craftsman who lived by math and logic, a man who could calculate and build things; he had to take up all the slack without any thanks so that she, in her mindless selfish too-good way, would blunder right ahead through life dragging and pulling and kicking everything her way, out of her way, expecting him to pick up the pieces and make it all work. Oh yes it was just like her to yank the door shut without even trying to understand it, without even bothering to see there was a part in the mechanism that had to give!

The ring. In her mind there was no such thing; its presence and meaning escaped her. So when she felt the door catch in her hands she reacted with her usual blind dumb force, jerking impatiently, annoyed, twisting the door away from its hinges. Of course never stopping, never looking; did not even volunteer a mention.

The man went to the door to inspect the damage and cursed. As if the harm would not be noticed. As if the blame should fall on someone else. She was in the bathroom combing her hair—typical. "Do you know what you just did?" he asked, on the chance she might relent. But she looked straight at him with her reckless eyes and said, "The door? What a cheap shoddy thing, to break so easily," flipping her arrogant hair. And he never knew it was on the tip of her tongue to say "I'm sorry," because that was another thing she could not do.

The man said nothing and went to get his toolbox an life went on, except for a long, long time he was at the door, never knowing how many times she had gone to this door to watch and wait and wish for him, desperately wondering how to make things work—why did that concept forever block her?—not that it mattered anymore, things had already begun to be settled, final, some time before, and no matter how long or hard he tried, he knew that there were some things broken that even he couldn't fix. They went about their business. Each went their separate ways, thinking their separate thoughts, hearing the door slam softly shut behind them.

Howah, this one. "Why do Indian girls say *Errrr*." Your barn door's open, you talk while you chew! Never mind Miss Manners there, she's too good for all the blood and guts. O.K. then, call it "Tale of the Midnight Gump as Told by an Actual ER Nurse," whatever you want wid it, that's my Moose Burger. That's my Fried Walleye too. Yah I ordered the Number 4 with the wild rice and pink cupcake and Number 7 with two frybreads, don't get off work for another eight hours. Come back at suppertime we'll tell you yet something new, sure, long as you go down to the Boozhoo Store and get us lots more. Yep, we work up a big appetite in here, this ain't a job for a pipsqueak.

Don't know what made my head swim and allsudden disoriented me like old acidhead flashback ting, musta popped outta my spleen. This little hobbit-looking old guy is just there in the ER amidst prior chaos in progress involving flying tings, screaming tings, big cops, plenty drugs and yet no homicide this week. Just there allsudden noticed him looking strange and outta place, a wizened Indian midget. Can somebody be so wrecked they develop an accent? The first clinical question I got but then his features don't identify him as any of the usual reservation clans who frequent the ER, he had these sly Gollum eyes watering, bloodshot, *drooling* red eyes and sly grin he said "Gump" and I thought he was calling me a Gump and calling me out, trying to initiate a physical altercation as they say, I took the Supportive Stance instead when he came into the gone-already ER situation room with berserk methamphetamine-coke-oxycontin-pot-booze-mushroom-eating-hyperspaced-hyperspeed-backwards-talking-backwards-spelling-screaming-numbers-and-gibberish-numbers-flinging-Land-O-Lakes madwoman all tied up ranting numerology and convoluted alphabets that appeared allsudden on the ER walls like post-traumatic wallpaper as background to this Gump, in the moment he appeared everything became very slow motion and distant, except for him. He appeared saying "Gump. Gump." Here he is making chattering tooth-clicking loud exaggerated noisy-noise, in some species like Owl it is aggression, along with this one exaggerated concerted facial expression and repeatedly pushing his hand, thrusting his hand downward in some sort of universal gesture language over his stomach it finally dawned on me saying "Gump." At this moment I could not even read the reaction of the other ER staff on this presenting case, they too looked perplexed and puzzled meanwhile other actions were taking place all over. There was input coming from all directions making

no sense whatsoever but the Gump strangely enough
stood in his own slow vortex of stoptime with two big
mammoth law enforcement officers standing there looking oblivious into space while the ranting l.o.l. madwoman
they had brought in hoisted into a stretcher in handcuffs as
a logical consequence of two befuddled EMTs having gone
out to try to deal with her and had come back in baffled
mentioning that the subject would be presenting shortly
"incoherent" for drug screen via the tribal law enforcement, sure enough she's there allsudden in four-point
restraints with sweatshirt on backwards inside out talking
like that too, nonstop even with IM shot of Haldol bam! in
the butt and it didn't even touch her. She's the usual stuff
talking in tongues, etc. spelling every sign or poster backwards and things of numerological significance to only just
her, shouting out her name with a bunch of corresponding
numbers "Get my chart gotta let em know I'm in here
gotta go home gotta cook a ham gotta hide the Easter eggs
for my kids!" is what she mentioned, shouting hyperspeed
having to be repeatedly physically restrained before the ER
door swung shut again and I turned once more to the
Gump not clear if these two phenomena could even be
connected. Police officers initially followed him trying to
figure out what he was, what he wanted, how he got there,
etc. but no response to English or any kind of Indian just
"Gump" and "No" is all he said. This finally caused it to
dawn on us he was merely Spanish-speaking with massive
ETOH overdose suppressing speech brain function, so
drunk you would have thought the little guy had crawled

out of the woods eating magic mushrooms back in there for a thousand years his eyeballs were so leaking bloodshot, then the big cop who could speak some for his Mexicana was called in or consulted. What must have happened is this: somebody picked him up partying down in the Cities and dumped him off all OD at the ER, told him to go in and get something at the hospital candy machine as a ploy, this is why he appeared clicking two quarters and his teeth together as loud as possible saying "Gump, Gump" but answered "No" to all the questions of what he needed or wanted, it turns out he only wanted some "Gump." Not the Juicy Fruit the Spearmint. Maybe so he could fool everyone with his minty-fresh breath, anyways then the law enforcement officers approached him in a friendly helpful nonthreatening manner the better to catch him with, meanwhile he had been a cute perplexing pet in the ER and this nurse slipped him a pack of Wiggly Spearmint before he disappeared. All this time the l.o.l. madwoman was a foaming verbal torrent, "My kids still believe in the Easter Bunny, you gotta let me go!" telltale expression you know that googled eye-bulge of impending doom like those eyes are trying to jump right outta her head and run away and everyone kept having to tie her up in four-point leather restraints which caused her to be even more agitated trying to explain more of what was on her mind but it came out indecipherable, finally the second shot of Haldol kicked in and she said "Oh!" in a nice polite even tone of voice. "Sorry, I'm so embarrassed. Can I go home now and cook the ham, it needs a honey glaze?" She was informed of all the drugs that showed up in her blood, urine, and pockets and sadly informed she would not be able to cook the honey ham tonight, "Where are we going then?" "Jail." "The NEW jail?" "Yes." "Oh. Good. Let's go." (That old jail still haunted by all the dozens of Indians who have hanged themselves in there year by year, the new jail reportedly so technologically advanced that not even one single Indian has been able to so far.) The cops said does anybody have any hospital slippers for her and they found some and so then she slippered away out into the squad car, good night. Sleep tight! but now I could stop talking and thinking all kinds of ways, the mystery of the Midnight Gump was solved and the law enforcement officers decided to get him into the tribal police car and drop him off at the reservation line, they drove him twenty miles out in the woods to meet the County Mounty at the crossroads down by Niibish then Smokey Bear could take him to the Detox.

O.K. then come back tonight we'll tell you "The Tale of the Forest Gump," because maybe that little hobbit got away. All right then, think I'll have the Number 3 extra crispy with no salad this time the fries. You be sure and make it clear who it was that brought us all this disease and crime and booze and drugs and Easter Bunny and Reality TV and what if I told you "There have been several reported sightings even now at this date," like you say in the news Part One in a Series (To Be Continued).

FENNEL TOOTHPASTE

I don't know how it could've happened, I knew her since 4-H. She never let on that the fate of little piglets in any way distressed her. Now we're in college and she's reading that book *Charlotte's Web*. She's curled up in her cloudy white nightgown on her blue velvet beanbag, so I want to show her how I love her, but no. "This is my personal boundary," is actually what she said. Next to her velvet beanbag is the tall halogen lamp that spills a golden disc on her head. Her pure white face gets paler and paler until it looks like she'll just float away. Who knows what she does when I am working at the brewery? Acquiring an alternative lifestyle is what I can't help but suspect. "It's a dumb book for children," I say, and I feel like a pig. The way she looks at me then, we should've gotten married back home in Sobieski right away, after high school, but now I'm losing her.

I can see it after the fact now; it is not a pretty picture. I know I'm beet red, a tube of hot blood and anger, a smokestack spewing blasts of pent-up words I'll regret. "You think your shit don't stink, you're too good for a

Polish sausage like me!" and so on, I hate to recall the words I threw at her in hopes that it would knock some sense into her. All those new vegetarian friends with the butch haircuts and tofu.

She could sure dish it out. The silent treatment, the way she ignores me. So now take some back, I thought, and laughed with crude harsh satisfaction. While I confronted her with all of it her lips turned scarlet as fever and her face got purer and purer and whiter and whiter and further and further away, until she was radiant and impossible and way beyond my reach. I dove into her personal space to save her but she twisted away and jumped up, ran off, locked herself in the bathroom, and turned on the shower. There was nothing else that I could do. So I'm listening by the door and I can tell she's scrubbing and scrubbing me off with her natural loofah and Dr. Bronner's Magic Soap. I can smell the peppermint castile suds foaming our love down the drain and it is all too much to bear. I went downtown and got drunk.

I ate a bacon cheeseburger, just one, with a beer. I went to another place and had a beer and a steak and a beer. I tried not to think of that little pitiful line of peppermint soap suds disappearing down the drain. I tried another beer in a different location. I tried all sorts of different ambience. I found myself at a certain establishment that caters to those who are out of control, with an all-you-can eat buffet. I had the ribs, the chicken, the meatballs, the meatloaf, followed by a trip down the street again and many many cold Pig's Eye beers.

She used to use fennel toothpaste. It smelled a little bit like licorice, and tasted that way when we kissed. Then she wouldn't. It reminded her of meat is what she said. She got her toothpaste at the organic food co-op. I went with her once and she was scooping up some brown rice and lentils when one of them, you know, with the stocky build and the hairy legs and armpits and who smelled like an ape in her flimsy sweaty cotton, ran up and hugged on my girl. These were two women. These were two excited women. They were grabbing each other and jumping up and down babbling about some concept that did not include me. I found myself at the natural toiletries. I found myself showing some herbal-mint deodorant to that henna-dyed orangutan who was grabbing my girl who was glaring at me. Who is gone.

She would sniff the air around me politely and then less politely though we never discussed it. At first she just left the newspaper and magazine articles everywhere that I'd have to see them, "Flesh-Eating Bacteria Found in Hamburger," "Cow Pies Eat Holes in Ozone," "Steroids in Beef Blamed for Shooting Rampage"—all the latest taped to the cabinets and fridge. I could take it. A joke. Then it started to get on a personal level, things she purposely looked for on the internet. This one guy could not sell his house because it smelled too bad because he was some kind of freak who lacked some type of protein or enzyme to properly process amino acids; he smelled like rancid meat and it got worse when he was horny, I'm pretty sure it said that. I crumpled that one up and threw it at her and even though I was mad as hell I was trying hard to be calm and understanding because of how she was getting so weak and wiped out on her beanbag with a severe lack of iron or protein that affected her mind. She was turning into a vegetable and I wanted to kill whoever did this.

I don't remember coming home or if I hurled meatballs at her feet or did something worse, and I will never know, let's face it. Because when I crawled into the bathroom with a massive life-threatening hangover in the gloomy light of morning, after a night of probable horrors, with the pigeons and doves all moaning in the window, there was that article all uncrumpled and filthy and taped to the cabinet mirror. And I had the sudden sickly understanding, so this is how it feels. To be gutted, and flayed, and split in two and hung up like a side of beef. Chewed up and spit out. I staggered around the place gradually getting the message: she wanted nothing more to do with me or my meat. I kept staggering around looking at where certain things of hers were, and they weren't. There were vacancies in the closet. The bookshelf. I ripped that article off the mirror and saw a wild boar looking back at me. I jerked open the cabinet and saw a small empty spot that was tubular and terrible and I heard a tortured sound filling up that small horrendous empty space with a groan like a hundred hogs dying, and screaming, and butchered, and murdered, and killed. She used to use fennel toothpaste, now she's gone.

Ms. Sybil Whiteside, major-slick fashion editor with accomplished clothing, hair, and accessories, betrays a slight start when she scans the City Art section. She sips a tiny cup of something fashionable while her sister Hilde's name is followed by comments like, "Though not landscapes except by suggestion, with their motile and strangely vulnerable (but never precious or cloying) curves, struck in harrowing juxtaposition to violent and stationary abstractions, there is an implicit power struggle in these works, a fervid sexual tension deftly expressed through use of place-icons." Phallic silos and Freudian grain elevators are mentioned, ambiguous swelling fields as well. Hilde or her show are said to be exquisite, daring, appealingly contemptuous.

Sybil's instant shudder derives from a subzero Fargo-Moorhead night in the mid-1970s when she and Hilde and Finley Fessenden stood on a corner of Northern Pacific Avenue beneath the giant fading Pink Pussy Cat, which even then would not light up. Twitching lightbulbs signaled the end of a row of seedy bars and hotels, luring them in with the promise of sleaze and decrepitude that they could try on as an optional state. After the two-story burned-out lasso-twirling cowgirl in hot pants came the lewdly winking feline. But every bar on the North Dakota side of the bridge had insisted on identification for the purpose of drinking. Sybil's underage face and manner had drawn the management's attention (with, she now supposes, some irksome, precious, cloying factor), causing this transit in cold.

"Then let's go back across the river," said Fess, though he and Hilde were twenty-one and could do what they wished. Over the bridge Sybil might pass for legal. Hilde seemed annoyed with everything as usual, how to get from there to NYC or L.A. probably writhing within her brain. Sybil often had the impression that Hilde had better things to do. Fess was Hilde's boyfriend, but Sybil believed herself in love with him, supposing him to be a dark handsome dopefiend visionary genius and sexual magician, though she really knew nothing about that, or him. Just: he was Hilde's, so she wanted him instead. She didn't take this cue to exit but instead let the next thing occur.

They walked back across the bridge to Minnesota, where the car was parked. The lounge that they tried was a romper room for freshmen, so loudly bubble-gummish that Sybil was acutely and vaguely embarrassed. Hilde's mood was worse and worsened as they waited for service and when she stalked off to the bathroom Fess leaped out of the booth and followed, leaving Sybil to order the drinks. "Pink Squirrels," is what she stammered. The cocktail waitress looked at her as if she were something wet or sticky that had been spilled on the table. "Do you mean Pink Ladies?" Sybil didn't know the correct names of drinks or why Hilde was ever-so-restless, insulted, and scheming, which looked quite glamorous, sophisticated, and heartlessly adored. It was useless then to consider the paradoxical mystery of Hilde. For some reason, all that Sybil was thinking of when the waitress arrived were naked infants and orphaned hairless squirrels that she, Sybil, had fed bottles and eyedroppers and milk to not so very long ago. She always took in small pets and recently bought her ferret Rimbaud with money saved up from babysitting. She would be a poet or singer someday.

"Hilde's cruel? Uh, I sorta know what you mean, she threw me in the pool when I was two," Fess had come back alone to the booth and in the conversation that was fumbling and groping its way across the table, told Sybil that her face was facile, beatific, arrestingly Elizabethan, that she should take some drama classes and be an actress too. He discussed her literature courses with her. The truth was that Hilde was far more kind to Sybil than anyone would or could be. In Hilde's absence, Fess seemed helically nervous, but Sybil only noticed this in retrospect, glowing as she was with his attentions. Then Hilde returned and among other things told Fess that even the drinks he chose were puerile, infantile, sexist, hurling one in his face for emphasis. He and Sybil threw a helpless look at one another.

Hilde blew out the door, briskly advanced upon the bridge that hurdled the frozen Red River of the North.

Sybil didn't watch for any recognizable signs for her to tag along. Perhaps remembering it was her own car they were driving, Hilde spun about. She quickly met with Fess and kicked him. She always wore mean boots and valued effect more than cause or dull logic. "Bad behavior will not get you far," is what their mother used to say, a teaching that Sybil still subscribed to. But Hilde was the one everyone admired.

Fess and Sybil had started to chase Hilde, but Sybil remembered first and stood by the car and waited, her breath shivering in and out in fog-clouds with the odd sharp sensation of her lungs being burned. It snowed. In the night those particles made a glittering vortex beneath each streetlamp, the spooky spotlights of this particular Psych 101 stage. Fess and Hilde were quarreling like actors in a stardust cone. Hilde walked away with Fess making futile grabs at her, his voice escalating, and Sybil heard the word *please*. It was quite a disconcerting thing to hear.

Hilde locked herself in the car and turned the keys in the ignition. Fess pounded at the window, which didn't break, but weirdly, fell straight down into the door. Hilde drove old used cars with artistic flaws and failures. The engine did not act with her decisiveness, balking as if to favor Fess or Sybil, who bumbled about Fess not sure what to do. Pulling at his shirtsleeve perhaps.

They both looked at Sybil. "Get in," said Hilde calmly and jerked the back door lock up. "No! Stay here. Let's go to the Off-Sale and get some wine!" cried Fess, or something similarly absurd.

Sybil jumped in. While Hilde continued to whip her horses, Fess shouted more disconcerting words including even *I love you* and *Don't let this happen to us* and Sybil knew then that she didn't know a thing.

Certainly not why Hilde remarked that Fess wanted to kill her: "Oh not literally, you little feeb." Sybil had thought of love as a solution rather than a problem, having no expertise. The engine fired.

So Hilde broke free even though Fess ran alongside her trying to climb in the window, dragging, falling finally in the icy street when Hilde smacked him with the windshield scraper. To Sybil's relief he was only figuratively crushed.

Would things have turned out differently if she had stayed there with Fess while Hilde tore off laughing, eyes ablaze with cold perverse glee? What if Sybil had spent the night with Fess, or if at the proper moment she had merely ordered a more sophisticated drink?

They never again went anywhere in any combination. Hilde of course did everything they all said she could not or should not, never came to the all-school reunion even though the mayor and everyone asked. Finley Fessenden, too, disappeared, rumored to be a cold-blooded CIA assassin and also dead from AIDS. Sybil ventured but didn't quite get there, except geographically speaking.

GREAT LOVE POEMS OF THE STATE HOSPITAL

I.

A couple of lawyers were chewing me up at the time, or I could have said something different. It is true the notion of "involuntary commitment" applied more aptly to me, the plaintiff, since I wanted no more part in this particular drama involving bad genes and chemicals and the comic inventory of threats. *"And you do love the defendant, do you not?"* The fact of our animal totems posted over the doors in the Hellgate County courthouse failed to excite any ideas of reference in this case. But as long as I was part of a conspiracy or a significant number in a scheme, there was no other way—

To glimpse the white bison. That one in six million million holy form standing alone at the bottom of this hill. To glimpse the white bison from the highest tower of this hill. To regain the pure asylum of a mind or soul or youth.

I can still recall that one called Lum down in the tunnels. "Yeah, great love poems, sell it to you cheap, a real chick-getter for sure." How we laughed at his ambition, a drinking cousin from up on the rez who wintered here each year. We passed the gray giant with the surgical bunghole in his forehead still laughing at such longings. While never a candidate for psychosurgery you might still ask yourself, what sort of animal must continually be lit up then tranquilized? Believe me, we are every one of us alone.

Then we arrived at the catatonic gypsy with her dyed-black Medusa hair and Cleopatra makeup, someone actually got her pregnant but is she down there still guarding the entrance to the underworld? These are coincident questions or stains that need to be dissolved.

In that maze of mental basement was someone crazy and horny enough to try. Life is a ridiculous scar upon a rabid beast! Meanwhile, we walked in some tripped-out adolescent odyssey through each possibility and to the door of daylight and continued on our way. Your path took you somewhere farther off beyond the bounds. All along the watchtower, old syphilitics were howling in a chorus. *I have cried enough in this rain. I have lived enough in this pain. The corkscrew worms of love eat tunnels through my brain!* Too late for modern medicine. It was the kind of day in June that was hot and still and green and carried sound clear down to all the sanemen in the town.

It can never matter what a former person said. Already gone for years and years and years before the court date. *You are my only drug. I have no home I want no shelter but the merest thought of myself like a wandering candle in the intricate* halls the weirdly ornate castle of your mind. Without this hope I would have never embarked on this obsession or the criminally insane trajectory of your thighs. My calla lily. My burning fire and ice.

II.

At the very brink of this cold, lapping shore Henri asked no questions. Henri at a place where there is no need to know any more than he already knows. And he knows all there is. The guardian of the brew is pouring chilled dark honey on this moment when we arrive, craving "The End."

Then we drink it into sight, although the view is no doubt different from the post that Henri occupies. I, on the other hand, might stay alive for decades. This beer does now hereby recognize the ultimate futility of words. Adjourned.

How else can I survive the foamy dissolution. And after all that, here is this mosasaur chasing me 90 per all the way from the Missouri. Just one snap ahead of his jaws, swimming the ancient Lake Agassiz for all that I am worth: the entire history, evolution, and cycloramic vision narrated by my brother riding shotgun or sleeping at the wheel. At last we are climbing up the Pembina Escarpment and out of the swift brown plains and there is nothing more that I can add (in regards to the strange days and psychodynamic etiology of the mosasaur, or the tremendous terrible tragedy of tyrannus oedipus rex. "You are not a shore that I swam to," is what the voice of reason said. "Drowning one cell at a time, not a solid matter").

It was a great volume of word salad and clang associations still echoing in the mossy green hallways with a heavy metal door swung shut and a lock click. The limnology of madness is a reservoir whose depth we cannot guess, just appease the mirrored surface. Over and over Henri fills the frosted mugs before we would ever have to contemplate a halfway. What good would it do for any one of us to encounter such a thing?

Vigilant, he tests the yeast and stirs the honeymead contraption. A thinner, warmer brew and I would never even mention prehistoric subjects or the channel of Lake Agassiz.

"The mosasaur will never catch us thirsty, by no means," my brother said in summary. Three black bears were rummaging in the garbage can outside the back door and I consulted them at length.

In the government compound by Red Lake there was a black retriever. Night fell and then the wee hours and the moon was skating on thin ice. If this big dog could be hugged like a bear, head-squeezed and ear-scratched into ecstasy, he would visibly express our gratitude for Henri's ritual beer. No matter how many times I threw away the ending, he bounded from the darkness and brought it back the same.

HAIRY BUFFALO

I t was a party town, that's why my cousins went to college there a year ahead of me. I wanted to study that night, but they talked me down to the bar. It was this rock bar full of bikers and druggies and rednecks and they were all white people, so I was scared. "You have to assimilate, Cuz!" they told me. "This is an equal-opportunity place. Everyone is crazy." They said I had to learn to cope with the rest of the population, but I saw that they could get a free drink that night just for bringing a girl. I stayed in the booth, waiting for them to finish whatever it was they were doing, with these big ugly Vikings trying to buy me drinks. When my cousins came back, I told them I thought we were there for "a drink," and it was easy to see they were hardcore regulars, and that they were going to be losers, throwing away their opportunity to get an education. They just laughed and started singing "Go My Son," which, in my opinion, is a beautiful song with a lot of meaning to it about a young Indian brave's quest for a higher education. But they changed all the words, "Go my son, leave the reservation, go my son, you're on

Relocation, go my son, take your medication." Finally we left and started walking to somebody's house nearby where there was a party, like they promised in the first place. This car full of white people came speeding down the street and they swerved up alongside us and stuck their heads out the windows and hollered "HAIRY BUF-FALO!" and I thought it was going to be a hate crime, but they kept on going. My cousins explained that we were being invited to a party. The car turned into a driveway a block down from us and we followed them inside. The house was packed wall to wall with people smoking dope and drinking and everything else with loud music and laughing and yelling and fighting. At first I stayed by all the Indians in the kitchen standing by a garbage barrel. It was a big thirty-gallon plastic barrel full of every kind of booze and you got a plastic cup and a dipper. People kept coming in the door with different booze and pop and wine, pouring it all in the barrel, which they called a Hairy Buffalo. This type of party is also called a Hairy Buffalo, from what I gathered. "What kind of Indian are you?" I asked this guy who kept getting me drinks that I handed away. "Horny," he said. He was all pockmarked, so I went to find a bathroom. People were naked in all the bedrooms that I blundered into. Nobody cared if you saw them. I went back down to wait for a ride home from my cousins—if they could even drive—because I didn't care to meet or ask anyone from this party. But then the bars closed and even more people and noise and booze and dope flooded in. I kept standing in the corner because I

didn't know anything about this town and what would
happen if they caught me alone on the street at night. My
cousins were still in the house somewhere; I should have
left but it was almost daylight. People were leaving or were
passed out on the floor. The barrel was almost empty but
this great big guy with a bulldog face jumped right down
headfirst into the bottom of the barrel and slurped it all up
and everyone cheered, *Go Mad Dog Go* while he rolled
around in the knocked-over barrel and they pulled down
his pants and there was his big spotted butt hanging out
and he didn't stop. Finally, he came out with his head and
face and shirt all sopping wet and he started howling.
Honest to god that's the way they all acted, they were just
a bunch of savs.

Once in a while an idea comes along and sticks on your mind like a wood tick. It could be a split-second thought of no account or usefulness, but you don't get to pick. It was the summer that everyone on the reservation decided to buy an ice cream truck. That may or may not have contributed. For sure there was the money. Also, it was the third year of a burning hot drought, and those per capita payments—"La Pay"—finally arriving a hundred years late. Combined with the constant angry fried-egg sun, it made people sort of thirsty and partyful I guess.

We had been breathing the smoke from forest fires every day until it seemed normal. You can see the next logical step, how the dust cloud barreling down the bush road ahead of you would suddenly part to reveal an ice cream truck. But they'd rather prowl the employee housing all day at the Indian Health Service and Bureau of Indian Affairs, with tinkling ice-cream music, pretending to be in a 1950s TV neighborhood. Employee housing being the closest imitation.

o.k., not everyone had an ice cream truck, but there was more than one, and that was way too many. What I mean is: the things that anybody thinks will make them happy, there's no accounting for it. Coozan went on a big long hundred-proof bang and landed up before the tribal judge. He was pronounced a lawfully wedded husband. I laughed and said at least he wasn't pronounced DOA or Guilty. We were startled by his wife: a big stacked blond, just like he always told us he would get. We were happy for him; I was the best man and witness. It was sudden-like; they went right back to Fargo, and nobody saw him for a year. Every so often one of us got a photograph in the mail with a caption, "Cooking spaghetti in our matching aprons!" and her flowery note cards about their "Match Made in Heaven," and gainful employment and how wonderful it would be getting to meet us all and then one day they showed up on my doorstep. Lots of people did, that summer of La Pay.

"Boozhoo!" I said, shocked again by the sight of *Li Blawn*, that great big yellow-haired woman with the popping blue eyes and *tootoosh*. "Glad to see you, please come in and have some breakfast," I offered since it was 6:30 in the morning. One glance said they'd been up all night, but they were not without a glow that now, when I look back on it, meant that they were still newlyweds on a round of visits to the clan.

"Why, that would be very nice," she replied and handed me a rosy wine cooler and plunked a six-pack down on the table, arranging herself in a chair with her big bosoms, which I looked away from pretty quick. They lit up a joint and were in the breakfast nook murmuring and mumbling little love stuff while I started up the coffee and hash browns and three cheese-and-mushroom omelets. "No thank you, I don't smoke the wacky weed no more," I told them, "but it's good to see two happy people, don't pay no mind to me." I was doing wake-up things like yawning, rubbing my eyes, and unconsciously scratching places or slicking back my hair and so on as I made breakfast.

So as I was finishing the eggs, off to the side there's this low lovey-mumbling, at least that's what I thought it was, and when I came to the table with two omelets and a stack of buttered toast, they were staring at each other transfixed and glazed-over with a very private meaning. While I was making the other omelet I glimpsed my Coozan feeding her with his own hands, trying to pop little morsels in like a mother bird to its birdlings. I still didn't sense anything amiss, I was whistling morning tunes to this epidemic optimism that had struck the reservation and scattered it with ice cream trucks.

I sat down with my plate and poured out some friendly sociable small talk out about how I was going to take their little children hunting and fishing and be their favorite uncle just as soon as they were born. I now recall that there was a cold beady sweat breaking out on Coozan's forehead. His wife had toast and jam on her face and up her nose. I noticed that she didn't eat her omelet, only chopped it up and rearranged it so that she could say, "It's just delicious, you are such a marvelous cook but I'm so full I can't eat another bite," with an expression that suddenly also told me *This woman is sure afraid of mushrooms.* It looked as if she was just being polite, but Coozan had no such problem. With this desperate mad look in his eyes, he began to stab each and every bite with his fork, gripping her with that low intense voice between the two of them, like in a crowded restaurant, "Hey! Hey look at this! This is good, see? Watch me eat this. Huh? Huh? Am I dead yet?" as he leaned up closer and closer, showing her how to eat eggs, right in her face until he all at once grabbed her hair and stuffed a gob of cheesy mushroom omelet in her mouth, smashing it up against her tightly clenched teeth.

She just sat there with this weird rigid dignity the whole time, while he grated the eggs on her teeth. Then he sagged away from her, defeated. I had never seen him deflated like that: he was the most gung-ho of all of us cousins. She was a goopy marble statue with eyes of blue ice that blazed into him and crumpled him into a wreck with his head in his hands, moaning. Apparently he was pretty near dead from trying to fulfill all her plans and wishes, but she should have just taken her pills. That seems like what he said. I ate my breakfast in a normal way and smiled encouragingly at the scene hoping it would soon make some sense. Finally the statue said, "Are you done making a spectacle yet? I have things that must be done now."

Coozan snapped his head up and said, "Not so fast, the wheels of destiny shall come ringing through the vale," shooting a strange sideways sweep of his eyes. I got the impression he had used those very words before like some hokey chant or spell. "We will listen for the bells," he added tenderly, and reached out as if to take the hand of the statue in his. I looked away quick. I got bit once by a rattlesnake, working in the oil fields.

"Well, guess I better get the garbage out to the road," I said, although it was not collection day, "and I better mow the yard before it gets too hot. Go ahead and sleep in the basement if you feel like it, it stays pretty cool down there all day." I escaped out the door, considering that if they crashed on the road somewhere, it might not be worse than whatever they might end up doing in my house.

As I walked past the screen window they were talking again in that electrified tone. That was maybe a hopeful sign; they were talking, not shooting or stabbing. I puttered around some after the garbage and didn't go back to the house until the lawnmower was out of gas. The can was in the basement, it was so hot lately I didn't dare store it in the little metal shed outside for fear of an explosion. I tried to slip in unnoticed past them and down the stairs.

"C'mon baby, don't get that way no more, we'll go make ourselves a teepee or go to Alaska, start over, we can live off the land where nobody will find us and eat that blubber ice cream and everything." He was murmuring low, earnest, determined.

One summer he and I had gone up to Alaska to work on a fishing boat and a canning factory. We went to this wedding dance where there was this stuff made out of Crisco and blubber and sugared blueberries that he was now alluding to, and they called it Indian ice cream. At least I thought it was Crisco, this little Eskimo girl came and dumped the can upside down and scooped out this white fat stuff and sprinkled it with sugar and blueberries. And Coozan was sparking that little girl and gobbling up her Indian ice cream. Later on Coozan told me, "No it's not blubber and Crisco, it is the oil of an ooligan fish, they squeeze it out and it tastes just like milk," but I just took his word for that. I thought he was going to marry that little Eskimo girl. He should have. I got the can of gas and came back upstairs.

"I think we'd better go," she said in a flat final way. She put on a pair of sunglasses and stuffed her hair up in a hat that she had been carrying and fussed around different ways with the brim. It was a Saturday morning and I had the weekend off from my job up at the school. After I mowed the lawn I was going to watch a baseball game I had taped during the week, and if I had to I would have invited them to watch it. Kirby Puckett would hit a winning home run for the Twins and I would jump up and holler just to sound like that or to restore my cousin to the world or to blot out this trouble that was brewing in my breakfast nook.

Then the door slammed and Coozan was standing there looking out the window watching her get into the car. "I need you to do me a favor, real quick," he said. I didn't want to hear it, I didn't want to ask what, but I did.

"Run outside after me and throw a burning flame, I gotta find that ice cream guy before she goes berserk." I didn't want to ask him, I didn't want to look at him, and this is what I got.

"Trust me on this, you gotta do it, she's fucking nuts, she's psycho, I'll explain the whole thing later." I looked at him to say that if this was a nut contest he would win the prize, but he hissed at me, "The signals! Can't you see what it is, when you were scratching your balls and your nose and all that it was a secret code between us that we were out to get her, to interfere with her destiny and poison her with mushrooms so the shaman could not contact her, and the prophecy of the fire is the only signal that can redeem me! Otherwise she'll believe that I was a part of your evil plot."

Then he smacked me a good right hook that nearly knocked me over. "Goddamn, you crazy fuck you broke my nose!" I tore out the door after him to beat him to a pulp. He threw the gas can on the ground and threw a match. The dry brown lawn went up in a crackling wall of flame. I was running for the garden hose as they squealed out of my driveway down the road.

Luckily, the fire department is straight downhill just a half-mile. My house didn't burn down but the yard looked just stupid all burned to a crispy black. It could have been me. I could hardly believe how fast that yard went up in a blaze. All of this put a different mood on the day, and I wanted to forget it. I went down to the Legion, half afraid I might see the happy couple down there, but somebody told me that they were out visiting different houses. My aunt, a trained nurse, told us that they had been in her living room and Coozan had asked my aunt quite primly, "Do you mind turning off that speaker, I can hear all my thoughts being broadcast." The radio hadn't even been on, but he glanced his eyes sideways, pointing at his wife in a way she couldn't see. And then my old friend Bad Egg Nahdoo told me they had been up to his house too that morning. "He said, 'don't do that blinking thing you always do.'" I thought of those mushrooms picked out onto her plate. I thought of all those secret baseball signals and the guy scratching his crotch and then I understood how it just sent her over.

So, that's all I saw of them that year. Later on I heard that he had turned into a codependent and now his mind acts like that too because he is so crazy in love with that blond. But other people say that they are just on drugs, like all too many more that have taken the speeding train to hell, that crystal methamphetamine, but they're still married to this day. And the thought I just can never get rid of is: for Christ sake, would I still be alive if we had been watching baseball? I'm damn glad I know to leave some things alone. I have my health and my job up at the school. And I don't know a whole lot more than that, or I wouldn't be sitting up here in the BIA housing, wondering what is going to become of us all.

JOLLY BEEF, MÉTIS LEGEND

(REMARKS PRINTED IN THE OSSIFIED SECTION OF VARIOUS
OBSCURE JOURNALS CONCERNING THE LIFE, TIMES, ARTIFACTS,
GREAT WORKS, AND GREAT NORTHWEST OF SYLVAIN "JOLLY
BOEUF" LA COUER, MÉTIS LEGEND)

1.

Would any individuals who ever knew anyone who
ever claimed to know, hear of, or to have caught
sight/wind of Sylvain La Coors, legendary Métis historical
figure & personality, or any of his dogs or relatives, please
contact me; also anyone who has any artifacts of him such
as his tomahawk, poems, muskets, fiddles, or snowshoes,
please contact the author who is writing the biography of
Jolly Beef La Couer, said to be half-Indian half-French and
half-devil, and one of the leading philosophers & oral per-
formers of the Old Northwest. I would like to correspond
with you; sing, jig, run buffalo, skin weasels choke rabbits
eat galet & boulets & bangs & smoke several carrots of
tobacco with you; drink tea and high wines with you, also

discuss fine points of history and probably brawl with you. If you have any information on any tracks left by Sylvain "Jolly Boeuf" La Couer, well-known hunter, trapper, poet, dogsled & oxcart freighter, linguist, bear-wrestler, and messiah, please write to me. P.S. Am especially interested in the long-lost Bear Naked Chief Woman referred to in surviving scraps of the famous "chewed journals" from the starvation period of that decade.

2.

Why have so many attractive, divorced, young-at-heart, willing-to-try-it-all SWM&F persons replied to my P.O.? I wish you all well, but please contact me only if you have accurate information of Sylvain La Couer, voyageur, performance artist & singer-songwriter, who is reported to have come through the area and lived in it several times, composing his now-classic works "Hoy, Hoy," "La Jolie Berdache," "Sugar Bush," and "La Bimishawin ("The Sailor," a French-Indian tune comparable to "La Bamba"). Also a visionary treatise on substance abuse, fur economics, sociopolitics, cultural mythology, race relations, etc. that starts out: "Arrived the Paix, Wiscanjack, Maccathy Mouse, Payjick & Three Young Men The Boisson Begun." If you have any knowledge of any haunts of his, any trees, potholes, or caves he might have hid in, let me know. Sylvain La Couer was a large, woolly, bearded individual who was into bear grease and skunk oil, wore a red tasseled Porkeater tuque on his head & three or four HBC blankets on his person along with various skins & ornaments, & tied up the works with an Assompcion sash that held his personal effects, which I am still seeking, including knives, pistols, clay pipes, kinnikinnick, dried meat, & quatrains. If none of these, then at least the rubaboo stains. Handsome, outdoorsy, adventurous, and good with his hands, he was noted in the fur trade journals and memoirs of Alexander Hornery and Charles Jean-Baptiste Shabbier, often in connection with La Tete Jeune Son of Sucre (the great chief Weeshkobug, The Sweet, or Sugar of various narratives), with whom he frequently philosophized, tented, and fought Sioux with. I will be leaving for the bush soon to do my field research, and will post another notice en derouine. I am still looking to buy a Red River cart pour la journey, preferably new, used O.K. if it comes with an ox in good condition or like-new horse; respond soon.

3.

Still seeking any information regarding Sylvain La Couer or personal effects. He would chase a herd of bison at breakneck speed while firing & reloading, hollering, singing, playing the fiddle, doing the Red River jig & skinning live lynx, drinking strong tea & composing poetry, sometimes riding a horse. Sylvain La Couer was a wordtrapper & marksman extraordinaire, an archetype who my important research now indicates did the actual running away with the Minnesota Territorial Legislature

Bill to remove the capitol from St. Paul, though it was certainly *stolen* by "Jolly Joe" Rolette, legislator and self-styled Métis flambouyant. La Couer has also been linked to Pig's Eye, the Métis father of St. Paul. He lived long & dangerously, was shot twelve times, stabbed five or six, scalped once, nose-bit, poisoned, hanged twice or thrice but never even trampled. He performed in Wild West shows and opera houses throughout the territory & was the toast of Paris, was une chose, our personne, qui marche avec le vent. Would be interested in seeing any manuscripts or hearing any songs in French, Cree, Chippeway, French-Cree, Saulteaux, Assiniboine, L'Anglais, Scotch-Welsh-Celtic-Druid-Star Trek, possibly even Bungi and/or Bungay but please don't kill me or the messenger.

4.

To all purported "Bonzas" "Bongas" and "Bongos" or reincarnated manifestations of the White Indian a.k.a. The Falcon who replied, thank you very much for your illuminating revelations; however, it is still Sylvain La Couer I am specifically seeking word of, though I would not object to news of Bunagees. I welcome any thoughts & advice from colleagues or handy tips from Algonquinists, Francophiles, Francophones, Polyphones, etc. as well as the expertise of any Saulteaux, Knistinaux, Bois-Brules or Mechif guides; in English or any previously mentioned tongues or else the "polyglot jabber." Also seeking famous speeches of La Couer, reputed to have said" "Ou je reste? Je ne peux pas te le dire. Je suis Voyageur—je suis Chicot, Monsieur. Je reste partou. Mon grand-pere etatit Voyageur: il est mort en voyage. Je mourrai aussi en voyage, et un autre chicot prendra ma place. Such is our course of life." P.S. Note my new address. Also seeking supplies of salt pork, potatoes, and grease-au-bread.

5.

While seeking to emulate & get a feel for my biographical subject La Couer, hunter philosopher & trader, I have expended 3 Bales Dryd Goods, 1 Trunk Sundries, 6 Kegs powder, 5 Bags balls, 6 bags Shott, 50 Pairs ear Bobs, 20 Miroir, 4 Bales Carrot Tobaco, 1 Maccaron Rum, 21 Keg Pork, 1 Keg Shrub, 1 Fan Oats, 3 Gunflint, 1 Gunworm, 4 Eyed Dogs, 3 Hand Dogs, 1 Awl & A Little Vermillion, also several mouse & muskrat traps. I have questioned everyone I met so far, plying them with trade goods for information, sans dessain. The natives seem alarmed for some reason & unwilling to admit any knowledge of the subject, though I'm sure they will come around in good time. I am hiding in a slough north of Belcoor, either in Canada or North Dakota depending on field mice migration patterns. I could use a commodities broker as I have now very few provisions & peltries en cache. Respond very soon winter is on & I am starving.

L ittle cousin, were it not for the wee hours you keep it
might never have come to this. In this lone nocturnal
vigil it falls to my lot to hear every shadow. You
know better than I how the ear of the night is. Long ago,
you nibbled a bean as you stood in a friendly moonbeam
on the teapot dome of an earth lodge on a bluff high
above the Missouri. Beneath a sharp black sky with white-
bright stars no longer seen in these electric rituals, the
wail of a widow died out finally near the scaffolds. It was
the year of smallpox. The drums of a secret society had
ceased and only the thin high whistle of an elk bull
floated ghostly on the bluffs above the young men's faded
love songs down along the big brown muddy river. Pure
night glittered in the smokehole. The village slept forever. Dogs would bark at sunrise, smoke would curl up
from the rooftops, until the last fire died. Meanwhile, the
village mice did revel. A dance of dried corn, prairie
turnips, winter squash, and pole beans. No wonder you
found the old night-speckled enamel pot in the back of
my cupboard an attractive cache for your collection: 1

pink Night & Day licorice pastel, 1 kibble, 2 bits, 5 chow mein noodles, 1 dog bone biscuit, 8 frosted corn flakes, 2 sunflower seeds in the shell, 1 dessicated crumb of frozen fried chicken, 4 yellow Puff Korn restructured hull-less snack foam, 1 vitamin E oil capsule, 1 elbow macaroni, 3 dried green peas fallen from the table, 1 dozen re-dehydrated rice grains, 1 Dakota Gourmet BBQ-flavored soybean, 1 Hamburger Helper "lasagna" extrusion, 1 blaze orange Cheez popcorn. True, it has been another long and terrible winter. How well I know your mania, cacheing inventory against the storm and the freeze and the daylight. While I toil at a clamorous silence I cannot help but hear you dragging the cast-off skin of a snake along behind the stove and then up into the lower cupboard. I heard you fill it with commodity pea beans and that crumby cornbread from last night. In a lost Plains dialect you scolded the lazy relative who danced and chattered the fall away but asked you for a handout. You shared your corn and beans anyway, just as you did with the little village girls who came poking with their sticks and packing bags in the long cold hungry winters. Mouse, I don't wish to seem ungrateful: share and share alike, O.K. Please accept as a small token of esteem and farewell gift this tempting blue-green kibble, brodifacoum 3-[3-[4'-bromo-[1.1'-biphenyl]-4-yl)-1,2,3,4-tetreahydro-1 napthalenyl]-4-hydroxy-2H-benzopyran-2-one, which I leave under the sink for your collection. So long, and good night!

I. was face-washing with a bar of pine tar soap which I. enjoyed very much in these teenage situations. It was a hard, sharp, rectangular black bar that reminded I. of a bottomless cup of coffee and made boreal suds. The faucet could have been a gurgling brook and a laughing waterfall if I. cared to pursue this line of thought. But I. could not say that sort of leap in fact exists. I. was attracted to natural herbal products at the time and I. noticed that there had appeared in the sink and on the floor some clear plastic objects the name of which escaped through a crack in the tile. They were the ring things that would normally hold together a six-pack. Then they were on the walls and ceiling, too. Thought I., is this all there is anymore to this whole question of existence? I. quit buying pine tar soap in health food stores when there was no more apparent danger from pimples and vague Asian wars, but continued to seek out apple pectin shampoo. This had something to do with a tempting Eve in a Garden of Eden pictured on the wrapper, in conjunction with the accumulated impurities of living and concerns about one's head. This whole incident was different shades of expanding rosy-purple in the shape of a spiky ornate cotton-madras paisley, and took just twenty years.

I t's just your job routine, to survive the mundane atrocities committed by CEOs with certain narcissistic, psychopathic, cannibalistic conditions. But this one tortures ants. Sad that there is nobody who cares about her enough to stop her. You navigate her variety of exhibitionism while eating a nice jelly Bismarck, deflecting her with papers. She beams at your reports, at her collection of little people nodding their heads on cue. One could be chewed alive in front of them. In such meetings a boss man would brag about something else, shooting elephants perhaps. Upon hiring you, this new boss made you stay up all night while ranting, scheming, pointing at flip charts with her stick and suddenly, at 2 a.m., collapsed sobbing, "I have nothing!" and you had to drive her home. But there she was all afire at 8 a.m. in pointed heels, garish suit, disemboweling a fresh recruit. This boss can't live without a number one assistant. This boss rewarded you with a trip to Hawaii and then made you advertise and hire a new assistant that she fired the following week after you trained in the "prettier, more stylish" replacement. This boss wants all the graphs to zoom up and down, like her moods, which is actually an easy predictable meaningless way for you to make a living. You already know her oddly juvenile repertoire of tricks. How she'll take different people aside, separately, secretly, specially, and assign them all to do the same task. Then sit back in her CEO chair enjoying the fear, confusion, jealousy, competitions. Then she'll come around to destroy and rip apart the individual effort, and someday she will die. But first it is time for the weekly episode: motivational speech, rags-to-riches Oprah autobiography. (Why can't you get me on her show? I'll find someone who can.) She is talking about when she grew up in an orphanage and she liked to dismember ants and have ant funerals and bury them and sing hymns and kill them one by one. Clearly, this is meant to impress the audience, but why? Her emotions rise into a visible crescendo, sucking all the blood from the room. Monday, you only need more coffee but they are a frantic mess of ants running away with the eggs of her perverse ideas. They scatter from the meeting, each carrying off a precious scheme, hatching all the cracked plans and borderline crimes of their demented queen. Those beady eyes gleaming as she stirs up the nest with her stick.

Auntie Grace says she has already been in touch with Princess Diana and JFK Jr., when the morphine drip kicks in again. The nurse came in and adjusted it and did all the other routine stuff while I went down the hall to the bathroom to escape my own pain. I was always scared by the high threshold for pain of my mom and aunts and swore to God I would never end up like them. I wouldn't have married JFK Jr. even, and I was right all along, look what happened there.

Auntie Grace says someday I'll change my mind but I want to tell her nope, no husband, kids, or church-sanctified life sentence for me. I do not care what all of you think about that. I went to college, got a good job. There are more dicks out there than you can shake a stick at I want to say to all of them—why buy the bull when you can get the ride for free. Of course I would not really say that to these saintly women who have frightened me into such success.

Auntie Grace is the only grown-up who ever took me to Dairy Queen, "It is good for you," she said. My mom never got to town or had a dollar for herself. I finally got one of those tall squiggly white cones and every lick was all that I had hoped for, around and around until it was time to bite down into the last creamy circle. "I am going to own my own Dairy Queen someday," is what she told me I said. When I came back to the hospital room I sprayed it with a fine mist of her favorite Vanilla Fantasy from the Dollar Store. I also brought her the Cotton Candy Fantasy spray and the *National Enquirer* and the *Star* and the *Globe,* I never saw any reading material other than tabloids in her house, but she was no ignoramus, she was "a trained nurse," people proudly said back in the 1950s.

Auntie Grace told me, "Little brown girls are the best. You are lucky."

Auntie Grace cleaned up after all the drunk uncles and sons and husband and more sons and I thought she was a doormat but she told me, "They will stop drinking one of these days," and sure enough they all did, even though it took them forty years.

Auntie Grace came back to the rez every summer to make the novena while the rest of us at the family reunion were there to get wasted and party and get in fights and wrecks. She just looked at us teenagers lying in the grass in the shade trees around the old homestead and told us, "God has a plan for all of you."

Auntie Grace told me the secret ingredient of her Spanish rice dish that was the envy and mystery of everyone that visited her house, but which was not a dish she ever shared at all the funerals and weddings that she cooked for. Auntie Grace showed me how to get the rice frying in the pan with all the hot peppers and onions and chili powder and bacon and hamburger and then she went around cleaning up after the drunks who were snoring everywhere and found their beers and poured them in WHOOSH like a magician, "It will cure a hangover," she told me.

Auntie Grace foretold the advent of the Indian casino when she told my uncle, "You will die playing cards and I will never get a cent back on your damn-foolery, so I'm taking my cut now" when the Treaty payments finally came. She bought them each a casket far in advance of the socioeconomic gaming development and my uncle's sudden heart attack.

Auntie Grace told me that she admired Jackie for "acting like a lady" throughout the Kennedy saga and then the Onassis years and finally this same terminal illness that has laid her in a hospital bed talking about miraculous tabloid scoops from the beyond.

Auntie Grace tells me that Princess Diana and JFK Jr. are not guilty of any of the horrible things that are detailed in these shameful books and magazines, that when the rare person is too good and noble and beautiful to be true, all the other lesser people will have the evil instinct to take them down and smear them, but that should never stop me from being who I am. And that the right two people will find each other someday and everything will turn out fine. Auntie Grace goes on to tell me the details of their heavenly wedding plans and I believe her, I believe every word.

In the state of North Dakota it is still not legal to shoot an Indian from a moving train. Rupert Highsmith, a lord and a fop, wrote to his friends in 1883 lamenting that he could kill only a dozen buffalo from the window of his elegantly appointed private rail car that year, when in previous summers he, with his entourage, had left great herds to rot upon the plains. The ghosts of a million beasts thundering over the tracks of the Empire Builder in the cold dead of winter 1978 did cause the train to slow. At times it even stopped. The conductor would make announcements about the hazardous weather and snow-drift delays and the bar and lounge car would soon fill up, as if this were an emergency procedure.

It is clear at these moments that the ghost dance prophecy will come true: at any second the earth will suddenly swallow up the invaders, and all the buffalo and dead relatives will return. This was just a pose, only people who were trying too hard would appropriate the ghost dance for artistic purpose. The passenger was a nineteen-year-old college dropout high on substances, hormones, and unregulated neurotransmitters, imagining herself to be the picture of romantic tragedy and the reverse doppelgänger of Greta Garbo and a famous journal writer. Miss Garbo, in a fit of histrionic self-gratification on the wings of mental snow, had decided to spend her entire college fund and Christmas vacation break riding the train, writing in her journal, until the train got to nowhere and there was nothing left. Somewhere in Montana there was a stone brick train depot where Miss Garbo decided to have enough of whitemen and travel back in time. She rode down from the big rock candy mountain, through the stark night into a dazzling white sea of nothing and nothing and nothing.

One need not have looked any farther than the Great Plains in that winter, the famous actress was in rapture. It was the most alone place one could wish for. The train plowed through mile after mile of sparkling pure new snow piled high upon the far-flung towns and roofs and trees. A cocaine night and a whiskey sunrise, with stops in wistful towns and stations where she had the urge to jump. *I am riding the hellbound train*, she confided to her tattered Five-Star notebook, *with a broken heart, a blizzard in my pocket, and a bottle of comfort in my sleeve. I am wasted by love in the wasteland of loveliness.* She would keep her broken heart as a strange little pet, make it perform violent dangerous tricks.

The bar car does not serve you without valid age 21 photo I.D. and so she had been denied by the bartender, a descendant of Africa who said, "Old Father time catching up with you?" in a silky mocking tone, clearly amused by the demands and assertions of another spoiled little honkey. There was train music, jazz and blues and Oscar Peterson Trio with insinuating piano. She had no business in the bar car. She flung herself upstairs to the sightseer lounge then, in order to sneak sips from a pocket flask and witness the beautiful night of no visibility and then the pure new morning. Nobody else was interested in watching snowflakes hit glass all night long—the skycab was empty. Miss Garbo dozed a little, hypnotizing herself, *You're dreaming, you're dreaming, you're dreaming, you're dreaming in snow.* When the train stopped in Fargo, she woke up suddenly, although its gentle rocking had become a deep soft trance she wanted never to arise from. Behind the train depot she saw the 1920s art deco Bison Hotel and she jumped off because she wanted to check in, but the hotel had been closed for decades.

Now it is springtime close to midnight and there is Thompson Red Scalp Jr. vanishing behind the Bison Hotel down on Broadway, between the railroad tracks and the trees just beyond the depot. A row of evergreens has grown there since the days of silent movies. Miss Garbo is following Mr. Red Scalp because all winter long she has lived in the old fading transient hotel across from the Mighty Wurlitzer movie theater, and she has discovered that the springtime is more significant here than anywhere else. Miss Garbo is an aspiring wino.

Early on, before the bugs come out, the green is new and glowing all along the river. Then the Bum's Jungle is a balmy bed with northern lights and giddy stars at night, a robin's-egg ceiling for the morning and something yellow like a light alive inside the darling buds that venture forth and open up, so eager and innocent, down below the wooden trestle. And then the skinny crabtrees burst aflame in lurid blossoms. Whatever they want they want it bad with their hot magenta cries and incendiary gestures. The wild birds pour their love songs out at dawn, every one a piercing heartthrob, and then that single week of hobo-heaven paradise is over. Great clouds of buffalo gnats and shrieking mosquitoes follow a rainy wind that strips away the fragrant petals. Mayflies hatch and die in the blink of an eye, absinthe-green confetti and summer festers just around the bend. Flits and jewels of warblers passing on their way to somewhere might return as deathbed memory. Lazy carp suck holes in the blanket of mayflies, spent wings clinging to the surface like a zillion dead fairies that nobody clapped for and believed in.

Garbo and her cohorts are near the end of Northern Pacific Avenue, taking communion with a paper sack of Thunderbird and a paper sack of Night Train, and one day soon she will be waiting on the platform of the Great Northern depot for a train to carry her off and be someone else someday. Perhaps a kindergarten teacher. If accosted by cops she will explain again that she is not a prostitute she is a poet and that is why she must be at a particular place at a particular time of night being a particular way with no visible purpose of employment. It is true that a search would turn up no poems anywhere in her possession, but a poet understands the absolute futility of words. She must be a witness to the final spring of Mr. Red Scalp since it is her calling.

And the ruminating locomotive, in its pause beside the station, has gathered up the strength to move its sentient freight. The train comes shuddering past, loudly blaring old news of eminent domain and manifest destiny as it picks up speed and thunders out of town into the shadow country. On Christmas eve of 1886 James J. Hill, the railroad tycoon and Empire Builder, bought his wife a huge Kashmir sapphire encrusted with diamonds because it was like a cold blue prairie pothole in the early springtime, ringed with bright-white swans and geese and cranes. On the Fourth of July in 1883 his rails reached Devils Lake, where the Chatauqua Train every summer brought people to obtain culture, education, entertainment, and the chance to safely see real Indians dance. Then the "Magic City" sprang up overnight, a tent town called Minot where a Métis bone picker witnessed the train crossing the new trestle when he brought his load of buffalo bones to join the mile-long pile. They might fetch ten dollars a ton at the railhead. A newspaper said that enough buffalo bones had been gathered to fill two strings of freight cars from New York to San Francisco.

The government issued notice that an Indian reservation could not be crossed, but the Empire Builder had his way with Congress and they authorized him to purchase right-of-way and the bone-picker's great-granddaughter crossed the trestle a hundred years later coming back in the opposite direction, feeling the train's long sighing vibrato as an elegy or lament for all that has gone and all that will come.

Now the Indian gets on the westbound freight and leaves behind his body. Past the sweet breeze of the wild prairie roses and the crystal spring and the holy rock and over the bones of railroad labor Chinamen, the train communicates by routes into the land of spirits where the sun goes down before it. Even the trains have gone the way of the buffalo, to cop poetic justice. And the railyard congregation performs an ethanol salute. The railroad killed the buffalo, pony express, stagecoach steamboat, Red River carts and a few heathen Chinese who were refused a churchyard burial and planted somewhere nobody knows along the tracks. And the rumbling groaning wheels of a hundred-year-old thought rush on over the ghosts of everything, a certain chain of churning syllables chugging through the restless sleepless ear of night like a blood pulse like a whistle-screaming 1880s iron beast charging down upon the grassland, *north-da-ko-ta, north-da-ko-ta, north-da-ko-ta* and all the thirsty poets here assembled know the total foolishness of dreams.

OTHER (EXPLAIN)

Document of Cession, Otherwise Known as Job Application

STATE YOUR RACIAL/ETHNIC ORIGIN. (This information is voluntary and will be used in planning and monitoring equal opportunity programs. Failure to answer will not affect your federal employment. If you fail to provide the information, however, the employing agency will attempt to identify your race and national origin by visual perception). MARK ONE BOX ONLY.

(X) OTHER (EXPLAIN): I'm a fully-processed Indian with official papers from the U.S. Department of the Interior Bureau of Indian Affairs, eligible for hiring preference or to vote in tribal elections or receive a five-pound brick of USDA cheese, pasteurized process, American. Cheese was unknown to my Native ancestors until "Li Framaezh" visited in 1801 with high wines and sundry. Chippewa women had been marrying the furmen *á la façon du pays* since perhaps 1608, but even though the new generations had begun to have French names, features, and linguistic habits (dubbing their full-blood kin "Lee Savazh"), they were still dark people who could not physically tolerate cheese, lacking a certain European enzyme and preferring bison meat instead. Li Framaezh went out of business when several dignitaries who had ingested his goods became annoyed with each other's wind in the council tipi, sparking *en kout feu,* which blew the works sky-high. By 1892 the people were dismayed to find themselves on a swampy rockpile with explicit instructions to farm, keeping a few cows and wringing out the curds to make *li crudge.* Some didn't take to this, and receded into the bush. Others ceased to be seen as Indians, owing to the prolonged influence of Catholic missionaries and sex. Which kept going on and on, with even more individuals of even more cheese-tolerating ethnic groups, so that some arrived in 1960 processed nearly white! Not quite . . .

PSYCHOPHARMACOLOGY

Well, I don't think I need the mood stabilizer anymore so I quit because I like my mood just fine, it's only other people that have a problem with it. Yeah, and I just need more antidepressants and you need to up the dosage since I never go to sleep and you are the psychiatrist so why can't you see what I see. *We talked about this last time, they set off a manic episode, which is what you are experiencing right now.* No, I am pretty sure it is attention deficit hyperactivity disorder and you simply made a wrong diagnosis, what I really need is amphetamines like Dexedrine and Ritalin and speed because you know I read all the literature about ADHD and I forgot to tell you that when I was a teenager and in college my drug of choice was amphetamines and I did lots and lots of them every day and it never even did a thing to me and I could calm right down and do my work real fast and clean up my room and stay up all night and ace my tests and papers and it was really good for me and that is what I need to do right now, to straighten up my life. *Wait, slow down, let's stop just a minute please. Let us clarify. You told me before that your problem was only with alcohol.* Oh sure that's what I mean, I never had a problem, but you know when things are going too good I always have to wreck them, even all my boyfriends, so don't make me turn to alcohol again because of the wrong prescription, but maybe you're right it's like you were explaining about that poor girl that was interrupted you know that movie and she had this borderline personality you know like I love you! I hate you! Help me but you can't! and sometimes that is how I feel. *Well then get out of here there's not a damn thing I can do for you, I'm just a medical doctor.*

QUOTIDIAN

At 6 a.m. the lawns of Elm Street were their customary green, decorated with plump robins and dew-jewels. A large, disorderly-looking mongrel named Peppy ran by and snapped at the birds joyfully. He was a mottled thing, somewhere between a prairie coyote and a terrier, with long laughing teeth and a tongue that flew out like some crazy pink guidon when he ran. His hide was of the same dirty-stiff make as the old-fashioned brush doormat on Fritz Lehrer's porch. Lehrer, the town eccentric, was already visible as a pale, glowing subject in the murky bay window of a tall-thin 1899 scrollwork white frame corner residence when police responded to the neighbor's call about devil worship.

"Mutilated sacrificial remains" had been discovered by Mrs. Odegaard and her poodle, who lived just across the street. Officer Nodak scribbled in his pad as they yipped and wiggled excitedly about "Cults!" Mrs. Odegaard had let her toy out to take a leak, while she hauled garbage to the curb. Then her screams (with startled mourning doves exploding like exclamation marks through the foliage) blew the prayerful-sighing elm-treetop roof off the morning.

The all-pervading spirit of the universe, the world-soul that moved in the life-sap of trees, was apparent to Lehrer. As a lad, he had run away to join the circus. With his first earnings he acquired a tin whistle, a peppermint-striped yo-yo, and a brown paper sack of horehound-drop candy, because sleeping in the cold wet grass gave him a cough. Still skinny and agile, Fritz Lehrer was now a retired history professor in a long cotton nightshirt and spectacles who was not unmoved by the caroling phrase of the migrating thrush, *Turdus migratorius*, as it came bob-bob-bobbing along, yanking worms. The incident across the street was not sufficient to move him from his vigil. (He could read an account of it later, in the *Police Beat* column of the local newspaper.) He regarded his juniper tree intently though taking peripheral note of the incident. He thought about the Spanish Inquisition.

Nodak had received the call at the Country Kettle where he and his rookie sidekick Torkelson were having coffee, pancakes, hash browns, scrambled eggs, sunny eggs, jelly toast, nutty donuts, little pig sausages, ham, and bacon. His longtime partner Pollack had died unexpectedly, of a heart attack.

Nodak glanced suspiciously at what he could see of old Lehrer, who had still been able to outrun him, last time he had been in pursuit. The white head with its shock of lawless hair floated in shadow with filmy white curtains wobbling about like a spirit. Lehrer himself was consciously immobile, a transcendental exercise he sometimes practiced in the town park, unmindful of concerned citizens attempting frantically to divert him. He stood in the bay window traveling through time, with a yo-yo.

His house had bay-window ears and a stoic porch with an under-bite balustrade, two deep oblong shade-pull eyes, and a stained-glass nose with bird-nest whiskers and a mortarboard roof. Nodak subconsciously heard two old schoolmarms scolding. *Put on your thinking cap Mr. Bullyboy, or you will have that cowpoop on your boots your whole life!* The heavy white eyelids would slide half open, one at a time. Nodak would have to decide if they were fixed and dilated, or lazily casing the street.

Nodak turned his attention reluctantly back to Mrs. Odegaard and the charred, skinless cow skull full of maggots that sat on the curb. The toy rushed at it suddenly and poked her muzzle into one writhing eye socket, causing squishy effects. Mrs. Odegaard screamed again. Nodak reached into his pocket for a Tums. He, too, had a favorite window, which he had been sitting in front of only minutes ago, with an appetite. The Kettle was this town's variation on a theme, a renovated version of a country-kitsch chain-restaurant popular in the 1970s heartland. When new, it was at the western crossroads, a vantage point from which Nodak could catch all the town's comings and goings, or the seasonal drama of sunflowers, sugar beets, soybeans. It had been idyllic.

But the town had expanded along with his waistline, opening satisfying new vistas of motels, auto dealerships, fast-food franchises, and apartment complexes. The Kettle had undergone expansion as well: large additions and a sprawling asphalt parking lot. That was when Lehrer had climbed up into the top of the gigantic elm outside and caused the town embarrassment. Nodak had tried to catch him when he sabotaged Winky Schmidt's Tree Service, but the old schoolmeister had scrambled into the branches quick as a squirrel and attracted TV crews from Fargo, Minneapolis, and even CNN. He was quoted saying that he had a supply of dried apples and turkey jerky in his pockets (solar-flavored, homemade), that the tree was of monumental historical significance, and that it was the largest, oldest, most noble official symbol of "our great state, named after the indigenous people who founded this village." Furthermore, when he ran out of water, they were planning to show up and make rain.

Then the tree became full of troublesome Indians and college kids on marijuana, mushrooms, peyote, and other wild threatening substances (but they must have swallowed all the evidence), and organized radical eco-freaks who had appeared from all over, and all the bleeding-heart clubs and preservation societies were circulating petitions about the "Historic Treaty Tree." It threatened to shape up to something on the scale of the conflagration at Zap, North Dakota in the late 1960s, or the rumor of it. (As if a feared Woodstock or other manifestation of the times was a-coming, the mayor of Zap himself appeared before the Chambers of Commerce of towns potentially in the path of the 1960s, with possible waves of dangerously demented youth sacking and burning their way across the financially dying landscape as the beer ran out following hopeful short-term economic frenzies; meanwhile, he aroused the National Guard with the portentous enigmatic code, "Zip to Zap" whispering through three a.m. deepsleep telephone subconscious mazes. For example, filthy psychedelic motorcycle hordes could roar into your town and out with local cheerleaders slung all doped-up across their saddles. So, at Zap, when an unlucky reveler dropped his pants to moon the troops he received a decisive bayonet poke on his ass for America, courtesy of the local militia. This could have been as late as 1972, but even then, *Easy Rider* was just premiering at Grano Fingal's Drive-In and the 1960s never did come to North Dakota, just the news.)

This time, there hadn't even been the hint of a rumor. Otherwise the right elements of the town would've been ready for them, running them off before the civil rights and cameras had a chance to get in and wreck everything. Nodak was galled to think of the TV cameras eating up those show-off speeches about the water flowing and the grass growing and the wind blowing, the damn Indian fad from Hollywood that stood in the way of progress. He had a deep personal conviction that God had placed the Country Kettle where it was. The Indians were never going to get any land back if Nodak could help it, especially not the Kettle's parking lot.

The historic-preservation fringe stirred up some citizens with talk about a "Treaty Elm Monument," and there was some big-city lawyer in a ponytail who had everyone bluffed for a while, but in the end it was a beetle-grubworm that got the best of that city-slicker hotshot. Nodak would have agreed that the Dutch Elm Disease was an act of God, if anyone had pointed it out to him. The tree was officially condemned. There were letters to the editor from crackpot strangers claiming it was a plot "like smallpox, perpetrated on the Indians by trading them infected blankets in order to wipe them off the face of the earth." Nodak was startled. He should have thought of this, himself.

"—and then that pickup truck full of Mexicans is sleeping outside again, one family rents downstairs and the Indians rent upstairs but I can hardly keep track of them, there's an old man they keep rolled up in a blanket on the back porch when they're gone all day, he's so old he can't walk I think, although they painted the screen black so I can't see him now, shouldn't he be in a home of some sort? It must be marijuana, maybe the Satanists, they used to stay out there on the farms but now menudo, tripe, and things are in the grocery store and they're everywhere, oh I don't see why they're not allowed to stay out on the back highway in those migrant shacks anymore, I could sleep at night when the Turnquists were my next-door neighbors and it's a ritual or a threat of some kind, they come in the night, can't you stake them out now and arrest them? It's not the first time I called. These are mutilated, sacrificial, animals—"

Mrs. Odegaard was already dizzy when her toy spied the enticing movement. Nodak gobbled up a Tums just as Mrs. Odegaard slumped toward him, deflated by escaping screams. Nodak caught her in an odd momentary posture resembling consolation. This was difficult, for she was the size of a sofa. In fact, she resembled the one in her living room, which he remembered when he and Torkelson took her into the house and laid her down on it. It was the same sofa on which Nodak had tried to make out with Mrs. Odegaard's daughter Myrna, when they were both in high school. It was squarely girded and upholstered, and the round wooden legs tapered down into tiny little feet. Nodak experienced a certain uneasy nostalgia in the presence of Mrs. Odegaard's living room, which was a sort of sanctuary of the late 1950s. Nothing seemed changed. There was Myrna's wholesome black-and-white graduation portrait on the wall, and the late Mr. Odegaard's disapproving countenance in among the knickknacks. Nodak went to the front door to spy on Lehrer while Torkelson revived Mrs. Odegaard. She was famous for these slumping spells and a man in uniform learned to particularly avoid her in a crowd.

Lehrer was still watching the brown clumps of leaves from his window, reminded of the remarkable soul named Cabeza de Vaca. He saw one leaf unfold into a bright orange butterfly and fly away to Mexico. He saw a skull-faced man eating fire as he walked in the slow-smoking traffic under the burnt orange sky and the toxic red coal of the setting sun of Tenochtitlán. The fire-eater, by repeatedly popping a flaming blackened white rag marshmallow-on-a-stick into the grotesque grin of his black-and-white facepaint, made his way up the clogged and poisonous arteries of the world's largest city with the shuffle of coins in a tin can like the clanking of shackles or armor. Cabeza de Vaca was a shipwrecked conquistador who wandered west from Florida all through the Southwest in the years 1527-36, somehow surviving and metamorphosing, his pain and suffering turned into a gift that could relieve the same in others. Thus his spirit was invincible. Through his journey into the interior, which became knowledge, and his conversion by native inhabitants, he turned into a helper, shaman, or "devil." He practiced healing, not killing, no longer a recognizable Spaniard.

Lehrer had never been to Mexico, but he watched the *National Geographic* show and had a huge collection of the magazine; he also read the travel section of the *Minneapolis Star Tribune.* The sleeping butterflies fluttered open in ones, twos, and threes and floated down to sip dew from the grass. Navigating by means of some numinous genetic map, they would migrate in eventual clouds to the south, perhaps 2,500 miles, never to return. But when springtime came to Elm Street the great-grandchildren of these noble butterflies, natives of Mexico, would somehow know to fly north. The precise microclimate or genetic hideout of the monarch butterfly was "discovered" in the

1970s to be the forested slopes west of Mexico City, whose throes of hazardous growth now threatened to crush the whole wondrous mystery forever. Lehrer wandered away into the cool blue mountains above Valle de Bravo where there were quiet chambers of dark green fir with millions or billions of butterflies hanging in leaflike clumps and clusters, the ground a soft rich mulch of fallen pine needles and muffled black-velvet-veined wings. One could walk in a blizzard of orange on a carpet of wings and know the meaning of grace. Or one could be greedy and turn all of this into lumber and toilet paper.

On the seacoast, three hundred green sea turtles were killed each day as they crawled from the waves to lay their desperate eggs in the sand. How terrible were the piles of dying turtles with their sadly blinking eyes of a poet, the old poet who was saying we will be very lonely if they stop coming, his bony hand scratching a turtle figure onto a beach-colored canvas with a wet paintbrush. The pack of craven mercenaries continued to shoot, hack, stab, and club these turtles to death by the truckload. They laughed and gestured at the carnage with idiomatic expressions to indicate that money is also green. The poet is the conscience of Mexico, said the narrator. If ever he did go to Mexico, thought Lehrer, perhaps he would bring back a nice selection of that special skull-shaped candy for Mrs. Odegaard. It would be nice if she would go down there for a holiday. El Diá de Los Muertos. Lehrer pictured her lost in the cemetery where the souls of the dead were returning to smell the flowers that their families had

placed there in their duty to dead ones "en perpetuidad."
She would see so many Mexicans coming with skulls in
the night. With their skulls full of candles they would
lead her through the dark in processions, to an all-night
restaurant where folkloristas played rare instruments and
turtle-shaped flutes. They would bring her that favorite
dish made of cow head. *O leap across the river*, sang the rov-
ing campesinos. *The border of Guatemala is a blue ribbon winding
into the tropical rain forest with secrets, but the Rio Grande is a door.*
From high in the sky, it did look that way. The narrator
flew across the verdant daylight into black night with
runners and swimmers caught in the spotlights or trudg-
ing toward sunrise with concluding comments and
music. "El Norte, where dreams come true."

Exhibiting a posture of great sorrow and pessimistic
empathy with the tragedies of the world, the elm trees
went on existing. At such times the leaves breathed a low,
distracted hymn full of melancholy and yearning. Elm
Street was a quiet, sheltered, archaic street with a pictur-
esque and condemned turn-of-the-century train depot
and a u.s. Government Indian boarding school both built
of solid, purposive red brick with antique federal-Indian
hollyhocks. These two visible grapnels of civilization were
located at opposite ends of the street, cutting it off from
surrounding decades. It had a Millionaires Row of two:
the funeral/furniture and grocery magnates' residences,
circa 1900, facing off on opposite sides of the street one
block down from the skull incident. The rental house was

slouched between the 1930s and 1940s, and aged about a hundred. Bertholda Fourbears would soon walk out the door and up the street to her cook job at the federal-Indian kitchen, because she was the sole support of a household. The first frightened five-year-old in her lineage to get off the train to be de-Indianized was her great-grandmother and now it was something to come back to. The nomadic ones are never done migrating.

Downstairs, the ancient José Antonio Volanderas floated in the warm sleepy air of the living room, just above the Holy Mary, Mother of God, whom he sometimes addressed as "La Morenita" when no one was listening. Loosely translated, the joke on Spain was that the new world stole her. Their own Madre, who spoke only cinnamon-colored language to the first faithful who did see her, walking the hill of the old Aztec temple. La Virgen de Guadalupe was the intermediary, she of many names who would intercede in their troubles. In honor of this miracle was her new church built on the powerful ruins of Tepeyac. Our Lady of the dashboard, cigar box, playing cards, holy cards, votive candles, 3-D holy-glitter picture, tiny plastic altar, every kind of statue. There were several of her around the premises, in addition to the shrine in the living room. José Antonio spent every afternoon praying and snoring by that one, La Virgencita with the sweet fuzzy doll-eyes, a gift of his son's wife Lupe, who had left for the beet fields hours earlier, along with Elizondo and their sons Enrique, Erasmo, y Jesús, and their wives Luci, Dolores, y la Rosaria and all their children, all good workers. They would not abandon a tired-out trabajador. José Antonio communicated through the Guadalupe his thanks and prayers for all of them. Also for this hammock. He could dream the whole day long now, and hardly feel his old bones.

Ay, it was true, they were peaceful clouds into which he was slowly, slowly sinking. José Antonio had been a small boy chasing lizards over the sun-hot rocks by the stream where his mother washed clothes and sang something that persisted as happy as birdsong, from a year with plenty of corn. His soul flew away to that waiting land with the thoughts of the white-haired teacher across the street fluttering erratically after it. Lehrer lit upon a bowl of Raisin Grape-Nuts, then upon the Viejo, who was the conscience of Mexico. Surely the poet recognized the ultimate futility of his constructions and yet he persisted, as did the shipwrecked healer. The last brave butterflies fell into the sky.

Peppy came sauntering up the back alley, looking for more buried treasure. He sniffed with great pleasure. Peppy was in frequent violation of the leash laws and he loved garbage day. He liked to dig himself a cool, covert resting spot under Mrs. Odegaard's shrubs when she wasn't looking. He liked to stash a few bones in the dirt for future occasions. With sudden glee he hurled himself at some lawn birds and leapt up into the air after them, descending with an idiosyncratic twist at quite a distance from his first impulse. He froze when he spotted the squad car, in which he had been an unwilling passenger on previous occasions. Through the divination of his nose, Peppy received hidden knowledge. He picked up the trail of this whole situation and followed it back to its start. He decided this cow head was a gift from the gods. Without another thought he snuck forward to reclaim it.

L um woke up down by the lake with ten hang-
overs and only one eye. It was the same
lakeshore where a crowd of two hundred
Indians had been partying the previous night until dis-
persed by the BIA law enforcement. It was in fact the very
same spot where Wee-shaw-kay-chak, or call him
WhiskeyJack, was walking along and saw a bunch of water
birds. Then he called out, "My cousins, good to see you!
Come on out of the water and join me for a dance and a
feast." They came scrambling up onto the bank, all gab-
bling with excitement. "Help me get the fire going here,"
said Wee-shaw-kay-chak, "We'll dance around the
campfire and have a fine time." Then the fat little ducks
and water birds went and gathered some tinder and twigs,
and Wee-shaw-kay-chak piled up the branches and struck
them into a blaze. "Now I'm going to teach you a little
song," he told them. It was a little Cree song. "This little
song will bring a surprise for dinner," said Wee-shaw-kay-
chak, "Repeat after me, and while you sing it, don't open
your eyes." Around they went, circling the fire and

singing. Wee-shaw-kay-chak sang a phrase, then grabbed a duck and twisted its neck. He kept doing that as they came around, smacking his lips with hungry anticipation. There was one water bird who heard the smacking sound, and, being suspicious, thought he would open his eyes just a peek. Boing! His eyes popped out and turned red from the fire and the sight of what Wee-shaw-kay-chak was doing. This water bird ran for the bank and dove down, down, down, as far as he could, trying to get away and cool off the fire that got in his eye. And to this day, the helldiver has a round red eye and never walks up on the bank.

Lum opened up his other red eye, and squinting in the burning sun of a summer morning, saw that he was rich. Everywhere on the beach and up into the grass there were shiny aluminum beer cans winking and winking. Lum got up and found one nearly full. He, too, would rather stay in the drink. "Here's to you then," he said and toasted the scene. Things are worse all over.

All of North Dakota is like a beautiful pelt, the tempting fawny and tawny shades of fields and swales and contours, and that is why I came here to establish my pattern of stalking and killing and hiding and fooling all of those who try to track me. There is almost nobody to bother me while I go about it; I work at night and even though the ground looks inviting, I keep low in the daytime so I am still in business. I wish I could roll all over it in the sunshine, roll all over the lush and lovely wild grass and the grizzled slopes and sloughs along the way. Newspapers are speculating now, people are starting to suspect and be worried about me being in the state but so far nobody has figured out I'm at the rest stop on I-29 as in KILLER STALKS THE FREEWAY and I mean rest stops plural because there is one on each side of the road, but they have been blocked off and abandoned by the highway department and the buildings have been removed so there are no deer hunters or birders or unwanted visitors. It is a very nice habitat, it suits me just fine, I can blend in perfectly with the overgrown brush and trees. If one of my rest stops is disturbed I can simply move across to the other until everything blows over. The newspapers are only guessing on my whereabouts and modus operandi. Way on the other side of the state two trail bikers did spot me in a remote area of the Badlands doing what I do, consequently the authorities hired in a professional bounty hunter and assassin name of Felix Concolor with his hound dogs and pack mules, but luckily it rained and I was long gone by the time they ever got a clue. Now if I could just roll on my back in the sunshine—but that's right, I better keep moving, the newspaper has described me as a transient mountain lion in search of its new territory.

STILL LIFE WITH "MARIGOLDS" &
THE BLUE MUMBLED EARTH

Today your reasons for living have taken a screwy turn: Because it is gray and cold and November and your kids missed the bus and you live on a hill with the town wrinkled up like an old potato in a root cellar in winter, you have to do it. Even though at the bottom of the hill the school is there like an eye, you still have to do it. Because you can't get anywhere in a straight line these days. And this tall old brick Minnesota school building is older than the town where you grew up.

It was some psychological corner of the Plains where everything was bare and square and laid out flat to just make sense of it all. Right angles would make it right somehow, but only by the use of imaginary, invisible lines could this trick be accomplished. White people sometimes went crazy upon migrating to the plains. (All that space perceived as the Void, previous laws & principles null & void anyway.) Alone with the sky they leaped into godlessness, just from the sight of supernal authority. The Indians who arrived there before them turned joyful, chased bison, and sun-danced, leaving their gloomy witchcraft behind. Phobic structures were few, you have read, and agree. Your apartment building and occupants are an alien experience you'd flee. Maybe you're Indian, a woodland Sioux/Ojibway, evolved with a plains I.D. There is some part of you that wants to make rain. It keeps kicking and running off on weird tangents, loath to experience this state of regression. "There were no wrinkled streets or forked-tongue trees in the way." You can tell it to your grandkids.

So then you're really skewed. Yet by means of the roundabout furrows you circled these topographic problems and finally arrived at the school. The yellow-orange Crayola-box school bus was spilling out kids like rainbow markers and color crayons in their bright winter coats. And you saw the children go scrambling into the play-crowd that sent up a glowing unanimous chant that squirmed in the air like a magical invisible caterpillar going *I'm happy, I'm happy, I'm lucky, I'm lucky, I'm happy, I'm lucky, alive.*

Even so, you're now sitting in the graveyard. When you woke up this morning everything you looked at was gray, and now anonymous gray squirrels throw objects down from a furtive gray sky that land on the hood of your vehicle with a very hollow sound. When you take out your binoculars, which you keep in the glove box for birds, you see that the clumps of birds in the gray leafless oaks are "Slate-colored Juncos," which does not surprise you at all. When you adjust the magnification on an 1870s yellowing whitemarble monument with exalted & worn-out details and a type of dark gray crumbly-rot flung across it all thoughtless, you suddenly see that there is a very specific thing that is yellow and exactly resembles a marigold. Or a certain version of marigolds, splashed whimsically over the tombstone just as they are on kitchen curtains, 1960s flower-power vinyl dinette sets, & the dresses your zany aunt wears. This is very unnerving. What kind of life form would thrive on the marble of tombstones? What kind are you, to be sitting on top of a hill in a graveyard looking at tomb-moss or lichen so closely when it is eight a.m.? It must be something else. You have only seriously considered suicide two or three times your whole life, never attempting it once. The color green as much as anything should explain it, since Sherwood Avenue was a gray tunnel with a slate-colored brook winding and curving alongside that you undertook as a means of skirting this hill. What you knew about geometry, geography, & a thousand yellows was meaningless in this fog, also useless. Then the bald slope of the cemetery butted into view so conspicuously green with numerous tall pointed evergreens on top that you thought of it as a season, and rashly swerved through the gate. That was the screwy move.

This does not make it springtime or summertime, you realized, when you parked by the tamarack where you saw a lone deer only three months ago. Next you drank up all your coffee, which is a poor substitute for sleep. If you don't have a yard you must go somewhere to sit under a tree to drink coffee, that's not good, you're asleep on the way. The tamarack is a somber & lofty tree, the dead keep on sleeping under its solemnly gesturing branches.

Caffeine is a natural stimulant found in plants, caffeine belongs to the xanthine group of chemicals, the first known users of caffeine were certain Ethiopians who ate a mixture of raw oryx fat and coffee beans. Someone must have to rake the lawn constantly that it may be so green. Elsewhere, you think of Frosted Flakes when you crunch on November oak leaves in the morning with a sugar sprinkle of snow atop and the freshly milkwhite ground underfoot.

But there is no snow and nobody visible here today. (They snore in the sheltering arms of the venerable conifers, only wind.) What is visible then: these huge mounds or pyres of dead leaves constructed by an unknown civilization. This frosted monochrome of granite, treebark, and the recently jumbled earth. A dollhouse church circa 1870, the various trends in monuments over history. (A slab of late-20th-century sparkly dark granite in November must be the coldest thing you could touch.) The evergreens that fold their wings down, brooding, like mother hens to the decently mumbled earth & the holiness of the morning.

The town spilled up over the hills not that long ago, from the evidence. There's a farmhouse with a red barn and corn surrounded by new condos. On the road past here, the one that you meant to take home, you saw a red roadkill. Yesterday, on your way down to Sherwood, then again this morning. A raccoon perhaps, from a glimpse of grisly guardhairs (call them silver this time). They are partial to corn, as are deer. If you went back down this hill and over the river and up the opposite hill to the lookout, it could be like one of those folk-art "primitive" paintings, how cheerful: See the county courthouse made of big yellow blocks with a clock. Put on a green-copper dome with a sharp Lady Justice and lay down a Main Street, down to the river where thirty-eight Indians were hanged all at once. (Make it look like a rustic dance or hootenanny, with a barn-bee scaffold & ice cream). Blue earth is the stated significance of the old Indian name of the town, but the old Indian told you it sounds like blue skunk. It has houses with wooden fish scales, lace, and gingerbread, like Victorian spectators seated in rows up the hill. Here and there a brick castle or schoolhouse. The churches, the steeples, and see all the people: they have neon jackets, not red wool, and no buckets of maple syrup or milk in their hands. That makes you think about pancakes, so you take off for home right away.

What then is the significance of this and the roadkill? The spiritual deer with its distinctive limp limped across the corn road one night; caught in the headlights it stared too long at you. This second meeting is not a good sign, as you understand it. By accident last spring you found the graveyard, running away from your complex. The path led out here with no warning. Accepting it as coincidence, you nearly stepped on a woodchuck. It postured violently then scuttled for cover in a heap of superstitious rubble that seemed to be its home. Curiously, a pile of memorial brush and crucifixes stuck with plastic roses. For unknown reasons you empathized with the creature and threw it your apple core.

Any day now it will snow and be your thirty-first winter. And although in certain spots the grass is far too green to contemplate, in your binocular view you can see that you have already outlived the average resident here. And there is a marble cherub standing all alone with chipped wings and false marigolds. The legend says, Our Darling Angel Aged 4 Years & 5 Mos. And you know very well that there are a number of planes of similar material with little lying-down lambs carved on top of them and heartbroken numerals, and you have every motive to live.

Still, life begs for reason and they continue to occur as you drive off into the imaginary sun:

1. The first reason is that you almost turned on the radio when you noted the whispery feathery hoarfrost of tombstones, despairing at the very idea of it. Anything to drown out any more ideas of your own. Inexplicably, in your mind you heard Elvis. Seven words about "Peace in the Valley," with a dollhouse church in some old TV ad from Atlanta, but like a tabloid miracle, it occurred: even worse things can always happen, you realized.

2. It could be for instance the corny recall of 1970s television commercial break special *Order Now* recording artist Ray Stevens on the radio; you could be in the South. If so, you'd fall into the socioeconomic marketing category of "fan." Climactic factors as they concern mental states are a consideration now, truly.

3. Instantly, you love the cold and all manifestations of cold. Even the sixty-below-breeze that whipped your thin red legs in their thin red knee-highs and short home-made dress that blew up around your short handed-down-worn-out jacket as you waded through a mile of drifts on your way home from school let out early for a blizzard, clutching your beloved books, you were six. "Ouch, that smarts," you read in one of them, marveling at this new expression, which understood so well that the world hurts you and you just get smarter.

4. You wouldn't take that dress code stuff now, what a dress means. Back then, your favorite yellow was the slick paint on new pencils and the long larval form of the Dacotah Paper Co. school-supply semi come to town and sidling up to the play yard, the particluar vibes of its rumble-snorting Caterpillar engine a friendly-giant rant in the dark slippery hall. Also, the carefree sun with spoke rays and possibly the crayon shades labeled "maize" and "marigold."

5. As a child you scorned Elvis and his fans on principle. The next stages in the process, including apathy, lead to the final stage, which is acceptance, the way one ultimately admits to powerlessness over other large, pervasive concepts, e.g., TV commercials or God. With that, your Inner Child jumps into the passenger seat, slams the door, looks at you and says, "Hey dope, listen up." It has two front teeth missing and cowlicks and freckles, and you are really astonished because you have never even read a self-help book yet you are a survivor and that takes it out of your hands.

6. The unreal discourse of the interior urchin/waif/ goblin unfurls like the preposterous proboscis of a certain Lepidoptera you once saw camouflaged on a daffodil, "these pigments being manufactured from their own excrement in the process of metamorphosis. Colors such as yellow, red, and brown are true colors in the scales that typify all Lepidoptera, while the blues and metallic tints are due to the refractive effect of fine grooves. Of the many thousands of species only 750 are found in the U.S. The forelegs of some species can actually taste—" you were reading as you walked along seeking approval and a blow knocked you sprawling, "Bug-ugly bookworm," your nemesis said. Shortly thereafter you won a spelling bee with the word "fratricide," and as usual nobody noticed. But ha! Now you hear what you want, which is "why." Someone keeps laughing like a maniac and it's you, you might fall out of your vehicle with the force of it, when you look again the Inner Child is gone, no, it jumped inside you. What else?

7. Although you hate pancakes your "significant other" is home to sleep off the graveyard shift and if you make him some pancakes, he may know why, too. "You don't have relationships, you take hostages," you heard once, which is true.

8. You heard it all in this state. (Minnesota Multiphasic Personality Inventory, "Land of 10,000 Treatment Centers," etc., you're surrounded.)

9. "Wait a minute bartender I still got a few undissolved issues in here."

10. Instead of on a barstool you would get old in a yard with a house, garden, air.

11. Back in the garden you met with a woodchuck; it questioned you with its harmless brown eyes, so you told the neighbor kids, "It's my pet." Then your dad came outside and shot it and said, "It's a pest." Oh here it comes, BOOM, you have heard about this part—rocked by that shotgun blast, you feel the sudden impact of The Memories all through you . . . peppered . . . "riddled" . . . "Them who don't work don't eat no potatoes today," was the answer.

12. Your pet dragged itself onto the road and expired. Oh go on, you'll survive, your mom said, and then canned nine hundred and forty-four tomatoes, not you again, would you beat it already?

13. Nevertheless you tried all your life to do harm to no one and to not betray a trust either, so you can say to yourself with all confidence "I am not evil and mean."

14. Only those kind get rich though, you guess.

15. Unreasonably poor all your life, you had a tumbleweed for a pet later on. So there is lots to look forward to, as far as consumer trends.

16. If you were mean & evil enough you could buy all kinds of toys for your kids and play all day long with them. They could go off to college blowing up bubblegum with no early influence of anything involving a woodchuck or the mandatory smell of cold dirt potatoes & gunnysack burlap, that is progress.

17. All you never got to do they could do, then.

18. So could you.

19. When you were eighteen you got married, which makes it almost like you're still eighteen.

20. So after all there is still time for everything.

21. For instance, you have never said I love you to your mother, father, brothers, or sisters, but in a few decades it could occur naturally.

22. Also, although Elvis could not properly be classified as a living thing, he continues to experience personal growth and to influence history in phenomenal, ever-new, and creative ways. You yourself may never be Loved By Millions. Yet you, too, could leave some kind of artistic legacy.

23. For example, in seventh grade you had a terrible secret from the world: you wrote poems. Then one day in study hall Dave Torkelson burst forth like a tumor, since you'd never acknowledge his fetid spewings or the malignant cells of his eyes. A smirking whitebread pottymouth who stared lewdly at you all year long whispering hideously about something he'd never comprehend to the day he died or was killed (better yet), then ran off with your notebook, giggling obscene loathsome gremlin that he was and would always be. Safe in numbers with the rest of his ilk he read your words, which were like the lone silk strand beginning a luna moth leaving the luna worm spinning all the metamorphic metaphoric everlasting crazy-loveliness of the world into envelopes, "defensive structures of no commercial use. The so-called wild silks are produced, for instance, by a species that feeds on oak

leaves," parachutes were made of silk and protective coloration is one essential thing that an organism must assume (your textbook continued), "she's a whore, I knew it, I told you, she must be a whore," he concluded, which brought you your first fame from poetry. Although you never wrote a poem again, if you visited your hometown you'd receive this recognition still, probably.

24. Another thing you have done is sleep in a flowerbed. When they took you to jail they still did not appreciate this metaphor or the nature of performance art. For one thing, it appeared under the *Police Beat* section of the newspaper and in terms only suitable to and for the benefit of the general public and its level of comprehension, i.e. "drunk & disorderly," etc.

25. To be unappreciated like this is characteristic of all great artists, or more significantly, with living ones, you have read and with no small satisfaction.

26. Perhaps the greatest work of this retrospective took place partly in the widow Mrs. Schimmelpfennig's garden in the black loam of midnight with you and your old Indian friend Dubby Peebles and a substance that helped you understand flowers & vegetables in a whole new way, as luminous tribal motifs escaped from their museum-case context. They beckoned you off the street that you ran down away from officers Pollock & Nodak & their guns. Belly-down in the sanctuary shadows of plants, you recognized for the first time how purely alive these things were and how they alone had a direct line to the ancient eternal mysteries of the earth.

27. More astonishing yet was the way they conveyed this, with a tentative leaf-arm or feeler-vine in the presence of certain teachable moments, mumbling "thus."

28. It was then that you received a sudden insight as to streetlamps. Beneath the beaming face of a heliotrope absorbing and reflecting the euphoric light of the moon (or a 1950s sci-fi notion), you could laugh about the two giant porks oxymoronically circling the square block and each and every square block of the larger square of the town, the squad car like a cute deranged toy frantically chasing the rumor of two alleged Indians on drugs. All this time the orderly rows of space-pistil streetlights were trained on the scene with a keen and startling interest, as if to witness a germinal implosion of midcentury black-and-white War-of-the-Worlds movie. And in the night-colored earth, the squashflower with its pulsating yellows and shape of an old-fashioned ear trumpet or gramophone kept mumbling old Indian legends and translated bones in the soil until it came to you that you were having a vision, and even though you could never replicate the first one, it gave you the motive to try.

29. But now it would be quite enough just to contemplate a garden, you would willingly concede, when something within you starts growling ferociously, could your stomach sound that fierce?

30. Ah so! in the course of these deep xanthic yearnings, you recall just what it is that looks that significant squashed way on the road home. And your garden would have squash blossoms and true marigolds, bumblebees,

butterflies, sunflowers, sweetcorn, and every yellow thing that appropriates & reciprocates the sun; and none of this would have to make any economic or other sort of sense at all, no, so you can go forward free now, because right now, this instant, you have come to accept and admit on the deepest level of your soul and your being what you yourself cannot change:

31. The woodchuck is dead. The woodchuck is dead. The woodchuck is dead.

TRIBE UNKNOWN (FLEUR-DE-LIS)

Sailboats off the coast of New England, tourist season with postcard-scenery and clambakes, and a blonde young woman wearing crisp cotton paused in a cool dark corner of the village museum. Her white-clad form suggests a sail in a lull, or a tall still bird that is studying the waters. Tall girl is looking into a glass display case where hidden things are brought to light. Absorbing the object before her and its fluorescence, this girl appears pale as a lily and gilded.

Gold bracelets and necklace, eighteen-karat orthodontia, a sheet of light descending from her crown: a shiny girl, and bright. Precious metal climbs up her long sensitive fingers and carved ivory arms in sharp elegant statements, lingering on the stem of her throat. The white-and-gold girl is a medical student at a white-and-ivy green college whose founding charter in 1769 promised to educate and civilize the Indian youth of the country, by which was meant young men of the native tribes.

Ninety-nine years before that: another charter issued, a preposterous scrap of paper by which the Governor and

Company of Adventurers of England Trading into Hudson Bay assumed exclusive rights to some 3,330,000 square miles, which they named for Rupert, the cousin of King Charles II, who was influenced in part by two French explorers, Pierre Esprit Radisson and his brother-in-law, Siuer de Groseillers. (England and France warred over fur until the Treaty of Paris in 1763, though Radishes and Gooseberry mainly remained on a side of their own.) In the shimmering reach of Rupert's Land, by the foaming gleamy sea, a lone Cree hunter happened into camp.

In 1611, in Hudson's camp, he was given a knife, a looking glass, and a handful of buttons. The Cree hunter left, making signs that he would return, and brought back two deer and two beaver skins with which he purchased a hatchet and sundries. He was no stranger to trade. The Hudson's Bay Company soon spawned a Scots brand of crossbreed to be the workforce and foundation of a vertical hierarchy that became the greatest corporation monopoly and colonialization scheme yet known. (No white ladies lived in the land of Rupert.) The French being similarly occupied, the new mix or culture dubbed Métis was often associated with rival companies. As for Captain Hudson, he and his son were set adrift by mutineers to freeze in the far north wind of Rupert's Land, in the cold and clinking sea.

By 1670 the Cree had extended their trading forays as far as Montreal, as well as establishing themselves at various forts in the interior. Autonomous groups of Chippewa had become consolidated around the Great

Lakes country and the Midewewin or Grand Medicine Society religion, which had as its purpose the preservation of the knowledge of herbs and cures and the prolongation of life. French-Canadian voyageurs were paddling the water courses leading from Three Rivers, Quebec, and Montreal to the Great Lakes region and onward, paddling the canoes of explorers and fur trading companies, singing their rousing songs and leaving their language and their names on natural features all the way—rivers, rocks, trees, trails, and children—guiding traders and establishing cordial relations with any Indians (especially the women). The following year, St. Lusson formally claimed for France all of the interior of North America.

(Intense competition for the beaver trade commenced, ending in 1763 with the military defeat of France on the Plains of Abraham. Around 1760 the last French fort was abandoned in the *pays d'en haut*, the upper country of now Minnesota-Ontario, but in the 1870s a group of Scottish merchants living in Montreal established the North West Company, moving into the abandoned posts and becoming a constant thorn in the side of the HBC.)

By 1770 the HBC had several wintering traders among the Cree. One trader wrote to complain of the frequent smoking, feasting, dancing, and conjuring of his hosts in the Lake Winnipeg area, but he was obligated, much as a modern diplomat would be, to spend time at cocktail parties (especially annoying the trader who knew the natives were only waiting for rival French-Canadian traders). When in Rome, do what the Romans do. Traders were also acculturating through such institutions as marriage *a la façon du pays*, in the custom of the country.

In 1869, progeny of these and other fur trade marriages declared themselves to be a New Nation, rightful citizens of their already-country "Assiniboia," which the Dominion of Canada intended to ignore and dislodge by purchase of territory from the HBC. The mixed-blood nation established a provisional government and *Le Comite National des Métis de la Riviere Rouge,* the flag of which was decided to be a fleur-de-lis, the emblem of the French Kings and golden symbol of medieval France. The lilies of France are said by some to derive their design from an arrowhead or spear.

That year a girl was born on December tenth and named for the flag that flew for the first time on that day, or perhaps for the order in which she was born, or maybe on some whim. In any case, "La Fleur" was the seventh child of a buffalo hunter and his good wife, who kept a little potato patch farm on the bonny banks of the Red. Her baptismal name was recorded as Angeline, and her Indian name was _____. Six older sisters went off to the Grey Nuns school and were promptly martyred by small-pox. The sisters shone down nightly from the sky in Manitoba, and told their youngest sister to do right in God and their people, for she had the gift.

Angeline was French and Cree and Ojibway and a wee bit Scotch. She traveled west and south with a group of hunters when they lost their country in the troubles of 1870 and 1885, known in Canada as the Halfbreed Rebellions.

Wandering down the course of the Souris River there were at least plenty of turtles and turtle eggs to eat, but the buffalo were scarce. A missionary priest met them on the prairie to say the daily Mass, baptisms, and funerals. One day the caravan of Red River carts came upon Ojibway relatives; for the parents of Angeline had been born in a place called Pembina. Angeline saw her husband for the first time: a fierce-looking Catholic of the soldier society keeping order on the hunt. They were married in camp, by the priest. In the space of two years they were reservation Indians. The people all around them were dying from starvation and disease while a relentless tide of settlers kept coming, hollering in greedy chorus for the remaining scraps of land.

There is a ghostly hornpipe wailing in the vale where Angeline's parents are buried. And the little baby . . . in desperation she had gone to the hideous old woman named Zwayzoo Nwayr, begging for her cures, pledging her own soul and anything she owned if only the baby could be spared. It was said that this creature had killed all the people in the woods around her with her bad medicine. Angeline held out to the frightening, feathered thing her beaded bag with its few coins. (Although like a mysterious artifact, this story has changed hands so many times, taking varied forms of clues and hints, that nobody living knows for sure what truth was meant to endure beyond the different speakers, families, rumors.)

The old woman snatched it as a crow will a shiny object, turning it over and over in her claws and cocking sideways her head with its bright black-bead eyes and harsh beak. "Ah . . . and so you, young fool, are gifted with the lily and yet you come to me. Do you not know who you are asking?" She fixed her searing gaze on Angeline who fell at her feet crying and praying but still pledging her whole being to the service of a witch. Then the Black Bird commanded her to rise and do her bidding.

"Child," said the old one whose voice turned soft and kind, "I cannot save your baby, but if you come here from this day on, all your children will live into adulthood and you will know old age and have many descendants on this earth." She handed the bag back to Angeline adding, "And you will learn all that I know. We are from the same line, but I will leave this world alone as I have lived, ever since my people died these many years ago. Only the mixed-bloods are left, and with their priest and with their greed they have turned upon their mothers." Then she flapped away into the trees.

A historian has noted the "peaceful army of the plow" surrounding the native people on their wooded island, on their hill above the buffalo plain, turned to wheat and grain. *God pity their patient waiting and appoint that it may not have been in vain.* There is nothing to live on but music, laughter, dancing, praying, religion, and potatoes. Every year for a hundred years, no money will come from the treaty but every year there is the hope for La Pay.

Angeline had eleven more children. Although she went out to heal or bury as she was called, the smallpox did not touch her. Not the consumption, not even the influenza when it came home from WWI. The mission bells rang joyously on Armistice Day, but all too soon they tolled for the dead. She would get up at dawn, help the children trap rabbits for a stew and muskrats for the trader. She would show them how to live from the woods and from the garden. They had a cow, a pig, and chickens. One by one, as they reached an age, the children went away to Indian School. They did well in the white world and did not come back, except to visit.

Angeline became the midwife, the medicine woman who carried her black bag into the bush. A son came along to learn and to collect the roots and leaves and herbs. But at age twenty-one he left to be a warrior and he died in WWII. First he married a white girl in the state of Washington and it became *her* grandchild, seventh son of a seventh son, who Angeline hoped would be the doctor when he was done with school.

But there was no one to show him his great gift. Mistakenly, he became an electronics engineer and millionaire. He heard one day that his grandmother had died somewhere in North Dakota, but he had never seen her. He had been told that he was part French-Canadian, and that's the reason he was "swarthy." The ocean waves lapped at his sons and daughters, and their little towheads shone. It is a land of great opportunity: he could afford a trophy wife and a bunch of kids who he would build sand castles with and send to an Ivy League college.

Angeline rode her buggy to Mass every day, no priest would think against her, and her goodness was well known. If she went to secret doings back there in the bush where the Lee Savazh were, nobody said a word. Her fingers were always busy with farm work or else the needle, thread, and Rosary. People would recall her team and buggy and alongside her the boy they called "Bay-riss." They went to pick seneca root and peeled cranberry bark and sold berries to the farm wives down on the prairie, and he would jump down from the buggy calling out in his sweet voice "O lay-dees, would you like to buy the bay-riss?" He was the seventh son.

In those days and for years and years she would go down to all the little towns and farms, all the way down to the train station, three day's journey from La Mountain. There she brought her wares, selling baskets of berries and later many beadwork things when she got too old and tired to forage in the woods. When her horse and buggy days ended, during the Space Race, she caught a ride with the Interagency Motor Pool on "official business," since a great-nephew was the driver. When she was a girl, the Sioux called her people the "flower beadwork people," and she knew the Ojibway word for this art implied the spirit in which such things were made.

Finally, one day Angeline had sold all and there was still not enough money for a winter cache of groceries from the store, so when the lady on the eastbound train said *How bout that? I fancy that clever little purse*, she thought, "I have outlived everybody and the one I would give it to as a gift is not here and never will be."

Now, here is the pale blond daughter of *Le Septieme*, studying this odd museum artifact, reading its description card and wondering, Why would an Indian make such a thing as this instead of something more Indian? And then *flash-click* she has a picture for her friend in the anthropology department back at college to try and figure out.

WOMAN'S PURSE
Tanned deer hide with flap and thong closure,
Lined with Bull Durham tobacco pouch.
Outer seams finished with white bead edging.
Green shamrock pattern on back,
Yellow heraldic device bordered in black,
random pattern of seven white beads on black velvet.
Beadwork.
H. 10.5 cm, W. 10.5 cm.
Collected in North Dakota, 1959.
Tribe unknown.

Twenty-odd years later when you motor into town there he is again at the stoplight, same as last time, sixth grade, twelfth grade, it's a wonder that they passed him: the very wet-chrome fishtail aquamarine 1950s sedan still in perfect running order, the very one, with his mien of a debauched nobleman, idiot savant, long and narrow dot-eyes. Never could read or write, but he's the acknowledged genius of engine repair and souped-up king of a thing in this town. Announced at every stoplight: the roar and spout of his heraldic chrome exhaust pipe, humpy-jump revving up that eye-slide, though at a glance he never did make it into the gene pool and thus perpetuate a dynasty—a shaggy unkempt blond with some inherited condition who is sitting so lovingly close to him on the front seat? No—when you pull up alongside, it is still his large hairy golden retriever. After all these years you come back to toss and turn and stare into the dark under the dear old log cabin quilt of a tortured adolescence, your mom and dad in the next room now a grandmother, a granddad. Faintly, at first, you ignore the sound of the insane proposition that mushrooms into your somnolent consciousness . . . louder and louder and closer and closer and you know just who is gaining momentum by the apparent change in frequency of a sound wave, the same auditory graph of certain fungoid verbal-sexual advances back in grade school, junior high, then high school: long fishtail body barreling up and down the streets at an hour they should rightly call ungodly, so that every insomniac must picture his medieval hair and continuous eyebrow and oblong-stubbled visage even as they view the moving picture screen of their bedroom ceilings, brain rooms, love lives, every sleeper and every waker too must hear the effect *vroom* through the dreams and shroom into screams of this town, and even in their slumber they have to pay him homage: stirring, whether or not they want to, they must know in their bones he is there in the waves and oscillations; they know who rumbles the street up and peels the night out and even you are subject to his powers, *Neener neener neener, you don't have no wiener,* the only magic words you can call up to fend him off until you hear him reach the unit of his disappearing and Dopplering away into what he always was, just a thought.

The sun came up, I saw it! After that I fucked up everything, but the sun comes up again.

The Light steps away from his former self and into another. A subtle line divides them. It is not a line but something different about the grass and the sky. The grass and the sky in each hemisphere. If not of the earth, then of some particular, individual brain.

It could be warp, the vertical stroke (though the grass and the sky remain the same colors). It is warp and all that warp implies. Then come *war.paint*, *war.path*, *warp.beam*, and so on to *warp-wise*, followed by *war.rant* or justification. Demented gods are playing with the lexicon. It is in the hands of an allegedly psychotic traveling vacuum cleaner salesman who sneaked into the big Mandan earth lodge at the On-A-Slant Village on the bluffs of the Missouri.

The word *slant* may explain things further and the slant of a cloud il-*lus*-trates them: the warp of each opposing the other. They may never again agree on what they see.

Grotesquely disparate, the two aspects of the Light turn their backs on one another, bristling with savage and comical energy. The schism is deliberate, stylized, obvious even to casual passers. The two personalities remain in this bizarre and enigmatic pose for one hundred and fifty-seven years.

The Light has been let out of an institution for the North Dakota Centennial celebration. (Nothing in the books to confine him. Instead they lie flat out, breathing into the still old air.) The Light finds himself in a darkened empty corridor, looking back on his selves. Hearing the click and echo of his stiff new high-heeled boots, he freezes, shocked and reconstructed. He scrambles over the slippery floor. He gleams behind a shadowed door.

The Light has killed and will kill again, if honor directs him. He peers out from his niche.

Those two Indians are standing across the hall. The first Indian is a handsome, sullen young Assiniboine in a classic costume befitting a brave and a warrior and a son of the chief of a nation. His stance is sinuous, yet solid, suggesting innate strength, grace, and balance. His shirt and leggings are of mountain goat skins, he wears matching moccasins— bright with quillwork in red, white, and blue. The shirt is decked with seashells too, fringed and festooned with scalp locks of Sioux (whose hair was lifted before the year 1832).

From the porcupine comes a symbolic crest, the quilled rosette upon his breast. A wooly robe of the burly bull is draped about his shoulder, tumbling furrily behind him, curly. The smooth inside of the bison's hide is partially visible revealing glyphs of war and valor. At the moment, the Assiniboine does not carry his bow and quiver or wield the shield, which is made from the tough stiff neck of that great unyieldy buffalo bull.

His hair flows near to the ground, with the war eagle's feathers riding it down. (Some stand stiffly on his crown.) Tassels of colors float from the feathers, while other feathers attempt to anchor in a wiggling nest of weasel tails all tangled atop his head. He wears something that is necklace and earrings combined.

His face is a remarkable dark red ochre, suffused with hints of virile yellow. Stoic, it does not state that he senses the presence of something mysterious, fateful, foreboding. Superstition and contempt reside in him at the same moment. So his lip is stiff with the hint of a curl.

He holds a long-stemmed peace pipe with a catlinite bowl, a statement of noble intentions and natural dignity. To the left of him is a painted depiction of the Capitol Building in Washington, DC.

Confronted with these two Indians, the Light feels his heart lunge wild against its cage. His eyes flash in the darkness and blood crashes through his body ringing loudly in his ears. He is perfectly still, but poised on the edge of mayhem.

The other type is a fop clothed in the white man's affectation and high-heeled swagger, facing a sketch of teepees. The extreme figure of cock-crow foolery, topped off by a tall black beaver hat with silver lace band and two-foot feather (red!). His period garb is a military uniform of fine dark blue broadcloth, frogged and striped with lace of gold; two great epaulets perch on the shoulders. The long starched frock coat is belted with a gaudy red-and-gold sash. Two fifth bottles of whiskey protrude from his pockets. A streak of yellow shivers down his pantleg.

His hair descends to his backside in thin little plaits and rolls and braidlets, daubed with greasy red paint. In profile, his eyes seem puffy and sated; he chomps a billowing cigar. His white-gloved hands hold no tangible weapons, only an Oriental pink fan and a blue umbrella. He rocks backwards on his high heels.

The Light leaps forward with a terrific war-whoop, piercing the air with his blue umbrella. The umbrella strikes nothing at all, for it flies open and yanks him aloft. Twirling away down the corridor, he takes one last glance at his selves, laughing the laugh of a madman. It collides with the blood-curdled air. The echoes bounce from wall to wall and chase him fiercely down the hall.

So as he speeds all awhirl toward a high paned window, there is nothing for it but to kick the glass aside with the heels of his shiny high boots while a song plays on the intercom. "Dance of the Sugar Plum Fairy" perhaps. The glass falls pleasingly, in tinkling shards, and the Light spirals up, up, dancing away, over the roof of the cities where his portraits still hang.

Although it is night the ground is awake, ablaze, writhing in its terrible electricity. The Light is astonished, but he has been astonished before. And he knows that there is no end to such astonishment even though a human being will refuse the smallest dose of it in order to stay living, and sane.

That is why they all had to kill him. He only told the truth, it was his calling; for did he not witness, in Castle

Garden, the ascent of a craft that carried pale aliens into the sky while many more, too many to count, crowded the ground with a chanting sound? And did he not live to tell the tale while his companions on the tour simply expired from the effects of this and other sights? These and many other truths he told when he returned to his wife and his people and homeland. For this he was finally apprehended as a conjurer and sorcerer, with supernatural powers to create lies without end, beyond the known capacity of any man.

The Light rapidly ascends the plat of the Potomac, the North Branch, the Cheat, the Monongahela, the Ohio, the Chicago, the Mississippi, the Missouri, and the Heart. Rushing, spinning, reeling, upstream and down, over hill and vale and city all a dizzy blur of dark and jeweled fire, the Light is flung headlong through storms and stars and clouds and banks of smog and filthy European pigeons, landing in a heap on the slope above the river.

The Light staggers to his feet and starts walking in the near dark toward the faint watercolor glow of the east again, looking for anything familiar. Then he stumbles off a bench of earth onto the railroad tracks, confusedly recalling the Iron Horse of the Rising Sun in the Land of the Great White Father. In his sharp, high, waterproof boots he's stepping "like a yoked hog," as his friend George said of him, but George was a rascal given to fancies who turned him into a ghost.

The vacuum cleaner salesman states that he performed a magic spell using certain word configurations and herbal smokes and powders. He claims that different entities reside within his psyche. He pleads not guilty by reason of insanity. According to informants, he has spent his time in the county jail ranting and raving the above information in a somewhat unconvincing manner.

The Light follows the tracks along a bench of the Missouri. The primeval river bottom forest begins to thin and vanish as the sun comes up on 1989. The state capitol building protrudes from the glittering carnage of Bismarck all across the river. Just below the railroad tracks the old winter Mandan campgrounds are packed with cars, boats, RVS, tents, and unknown sleeping people. Teetering on the brink of civilization, the Light proceeds under cover to the possible refuge of the earth lodge village on the hill. Finding it to be yet another deserted museum, the Light approaches the center smoke hole and its shaft of pure light where he may implore his gods for an ending. Just then, from the shadows and the historically accurate reconstructed chief's bed, he hears the voice of the veteran vacuum cleaner salesman in its initial pitch always suited to the particular circumstances, "Care to join me for a drink?"

After the initial introduction, mainly conducted in sign language, whereby the salesman indicated, "I could not help but notice that you had two jugs and there are two of us." The two men's stories are exchanged, and this questionable subject, the vacuum cleaner salesman, who is either a genuine case or a very persistent malingerer, explained about the entities now battling within him. In the course of the libations he had enlisted the Light in a friendly way as a potential business partner and tourist attraction. This he claims to have accomplished by means of the Vulcan Mind-Meld, of which he was an accomplished master.

He explained that this visible manifestation of the Light, after undergoing the Vulcan Mind-Meld, stepped into the shaft of sunlight coming through the smoke hole of the Mandan earth lodge and was transported or beamed up to wherever he had come from.

"Wi-jun-jon he walked among us, though only some of us could see him," he elaborated.

He related in some fashion the story of the Light, a.k.a. Wi-jun-jon, The Pigeon's Egg head, and of his journey to Washington, DC to meet the president and to see for himself how many white people there were on shore now and what they were doing in their chief's town. He told his people that he had tried to keep a count of the white people by notching marks on sticks for every white man's house he saw, but finally had to throw the sticks away long before the tribal delegation even reached St. Louis. He told them of the belief and behaviors and costumes and customs of Washington society, including the ladies whose darling and honored guest he was at many fancy parties; he whistled the tune "Yankee Doodle" for his audience, and performed numerous other tricks and manners; he repeatedly informed them of the white man's forts and gunships and cannons, and the marvels of the U.S. Patent Office. After three years he was still not done with the report, and so his "lying medicine" was deemed too great and fearsome, so he was ceremonially executed by the shamans.

However, it is the "lying medicine" of this accused vacuum cleaner salesman with which we must now concern ourselves. He is currently under investigation for posing and scamming in various other venues. It appears that several different incidents may be connected to this poseur. At the time of this last incident he had been passing himself off as a Hawaiian king to a group of rich old ladies whose interest in the subject he had gleaned from his voluminous and speedy casing of a town's newspapers and habits. They invested their funds in his schemes as well as purchased top-of-the-line vacuum cleaners to begin with, or what they believed to be such. Remarkably, although they were a group of tight German farm widows, he was able to convince them all that their houses were filthy because they did not own the right vacuum cleaner. Anybody over here would have seen he was just an extra-special-bad Indian with his bag of tricks. Later, he and his now-missing partner tried interesting some folks in a local bar into a product demonstration including a comely lady to whom he offered to show his crevice tool. They repaired to her residence for the demonstration. Sometime later, her husband returned to the residence, which is when this subject fled and apparently sought lodging in the earth lodge on the hill. At this time he says he was in town and had an important appointment up at the state capitol building where he was to cement a huge sales contract for cleaning up after the Party of the Century, which was kicking off that very week. He explained the technicalities of the laser show to be projected onto the state skyscraper. He was extremely verbal and disjointed, touching on other subjects of which he was said to have encyclopedic knowledge. He explained that he was a scholar and historical reenactor, and that he was in character much of the time and could not be bothered with distracting details of reality. He explained several other ways in which he was an honored cultural ambassador to the North Dakota centennial and refused to answer any further questions, only stating, "Wi-jun-jon he walks among us, he may knock at your door."

George Catlin. *Wi-jun-jon (The Pigeon's Egg Head) On His Way Home from Washington, DC.*

1832

Pen and ink, 13 3/4" x 10"

Newberry Library, Chicago, Illinois

Edward E. Ayer Collection

George Catlin. *Ah Jon-Jon, The Light, Going to and Returning from Washington.* Oil on canvas. Collection of the Smithsonian Institution, Washington, DC.

1974; ref. "Letters and Notes on the Manners, Customs, and Conditions of the North American Indian, Written During Eight Years' Travel (1832-1839) Amongst the Wildest Tribes of Indians in North America," By George Catlin, Volume II.

In the morning he brushes my hair down my bare back, like a mane, and plaits it into a braid. We sit in the bed till daylight comes seeping through all its filters, making a waterfall pool on the floor. There we put our bare feet, warming up. The coffee is going and the house is still, quiet, and he says nice things to me. Even in French, one that sounds like "L'Blonde." Palomino, he whispers, you big golden thing, you're ma love XLT, the way we run together is strong, wild, and free. If we lived in the old-time days in every sunrise glow of our teepee, there we'd be, he'd paint the part red on my head so everyone could see, just that easy, that there is someone who loves me. He would paint my face, too. If I had to go out in the harsh cold wind or the hot dusty sun, he'd even plaster my face with grease and paint, and I'd know for certain what a store he set by just looking at me. That's what he told me, that's how it is. He braids my hair, and then I braid his.

When we made that walk down the aisle together I felt everything soaring, expanding, and I felt sorry for the small helpless thoughts when we walked through the door: oh-too-good-to-be-true hunk of a lusty sensitive Indian brave, will you fall off your wagon and drink up my check? Take up my space, fence me in? Call me names.

Beat me up. Maybe knives. As if it were that deadly fasci-
nating snake in candy-striped colors, it came sliding
through my mind, room to room, lightning-swift, and it
struck: my ex and his lowdown slithering hate, how he
lied. All the pretty candystick, very-sick, really-slick and
quick-changing lies, how they squeezed my lungs slowly
and stealthily blow by blow, bit by bit, "you're so beautiful, beautiful" then "you slop-brain, you pig," so finally I
liked it, loved it, when he came at me with cutlery, my
brand-new anniversary gift set. It was a good quality of
stainless steel, extra sharp. At last, I could see it, grab it,
stab it, the truth! And he was running with his plastic
movie-mannequin face all melting off, the lizard alien
underneath scrambling and hissing from room to room
leaking its nasty toxic blood all over "luxury apartment"
as they said in the report, "all in shambles," "ransacked,"
and "turned upside down," as even my underwear were
blamed. Always hunting for excuses, evidence, he held
them up in the air, his slight tongue-flicking reptile-eyed
movements a prelude to doom, a silent tick in dead time.

With a nuclear scream he ripped them in two, so I felt
divorced. Everything happened, those knives. All this
starting with a "special candlelight dinner," then there it
was, across the table seething with vile liquid biochemical
explosions as I reached for another helping of potatoes
lyonnaise and smiled and suddenly I was "screwing his
boss," "taking him for granted," "trying to pussywhip," "be
better than," "make a fool of," and obviously provoke him,
"so now you're going to pay." All the while he's hiding in

the shell of a human, saying how lovely your extra-large tits are, now they're "cows," and he's scaly, an alien, something stingy and hideous you have to get away from, quick, quick.

Marriage is too-too scary, I said to my brave. He said, I know. Still, we went ahead with the move, me attempting to hide my uneasy thoughts. Hey, it don't matter, it's O.K., I don't blame you, his curly eyes laughed when I glanced up at him and we stood side by side. This is us. Forget about that measly squirt and his bathroom scales. Your wish is my pleasure, he meant when he grinned extra-wide, took out his fat bingo wallet and his eyes went like two upside-down smiles, and ooh! I just love that, all those large white Indian teeth like hominy. Go ahead, don't be bashful, he likes to say. He's more than just big, he's . . . XXXL. His strong manly heart. How he thinks, what he does, he heaps unto me his noble and generous savage wild extra-extra love.

He picked up our shopping cart and braced it thoughtfully against the shelf, started stacking #10 cans like a foundation to the household we were now going to share. I didn't stop him, tell him it was really not more economical, that other small details usually must figure in. He meant business, plain to see: the two of us moving in together meant serious groceries. We happened to be at the giant-size stuff in Aisle One, that didn't faze him. In went gallon cans of corn niblets, kidney and pinto and Great Northern beans, stewed tomatoes, small potatoes, solid pack pumpkin and spiced apple rings. Red Indian River grapefruit sections in natural juices, my personal favorite, not his—not even! He's into heavy syrup. Laid in a stock of yellow cling peach halves and diced Bartlett pears, several gallons of Premium Food Service Chili Con Carne and the Chef's ravioli, then looked with a strange startled expression at Wigwam Brand Cooked Wild Rice, put that in too.

Maybe his people buy groceries this way, don't know. Though generosity is an Indian virtue, I'm told—they like to eat in huge festive bunches, the whole village, neighbors, relatives, and anyone when anything happens to celebrate and feast. Maybe they're coming to dinner soon, I hope so, can't wait. It *will* be so great. All day long we'll boil things in pots, I'm going to go buy some great big ones, right off—at night they'll be rolled up in blankets all over the furniture and floor sleeping, we'll have company, be happy. We have this radar love . . . the second I think "frybread," there he is hauling down a fifty-pound can of Spry, that shortening with the maniacal elf. I think he does seem kind of lonesome looking at the label on those gallon cans of wild rice: black background, jump-out-at-you-bright scene of a solitary Indian man paddling his canoe into a squiggly sunset like a big red-and-orange hot-air balloon slumping into the remote sky-blue waters, bubbling flames. On the shores, the cool dark green pines must be whispering something home-sick, *Min-ne-so-ta, Min-ne-so-ta* . . . the reeds and grasses rustling a heartfelt refrain.

Or, maybe these giant foodstuffs are the only type he's familiar with, as far as preparation methods. Maybe the only way he knows how to cook is for larger foodservice populations, larger than two, say a cellblock.

A restaurant.

An elementary school, I could see that. Like their laid-back favorite uncle, he'd be there for them, patiently extending his huge ice-cream scoop of potatoes and gravy toward their beaming little faces, mean jokes. Maybe he just likes to get the job done and get it done big, so there's no risk of empties, disappointments. Something tells me he doesn't plan to get out of the house again for food supplies, not real soon. The reason he stays inside all day and only goes out at night, I mean it's obvious, he's establishing commitment. A routine. He has to sleep in the daytime, get a job at night, just so we can be together. What it is, is a pattern. We'll have the whole store to ourselves at 2 or 3 a.m. next time.

All the pretty coralsnake, candystick—

Something tells me that underneath everything, as the layers come off day by day, until the day we're both irreversibly naked and natural with one another getting showered and dressed for an important occasion, he is never going to come foaming at me like some low-budget horror-show waving a bathroom scale "trying to sneak some on huh, what do you weigh now, get on here," until there's nothing left to do but poke him in the balls with a toilet plunger, pop his creepy-dirty bad mouth. That won't happen. My ex was what I said he was, just a damn intruder. While he was groaning on the floor like a cheap TV movie, I was trying to get my clothes on and get out and all this time he's crawling after me dragging himself, hooking his claws in my tricot-lace slip, even after I took away the scale and banged him on the head with it one-two-three, still he kept coming like a cable-TV nightmare till I threw the chicken cacciatore on him and spaghetti and even the lasagna, what a waste. There were people coming over for dinner, he'd do anything to wreck my appetite, disgrace me. One last glimpse of him worming along maliciously, with those steaming-red noodle-guts trailing behind him and I ran off slamming doors before a chainsaw or something came poking through, or a pitch-fork, that's how scared of him I was, I was crazy. I was running away down the sidewalk with only a scream on. When finally I dared confess this, all my Indian man did was look slightly mystical at the ending, a terrible moment, and he sighed, "Dang, that must of been a spectacular sight, how'd I miss it?" and we laughed and suddenly, like that, that whole thing was over.

As we move along he picks up a four-and-a-half-pound can of tuna fish with the slinky-cute mermaid you don't notice on the regular-size label. He stacks up fifty-four pounds of that, a whole lot of hotdish. "Better get some Norwegian food," he jokes. He must have a big family. I picture a couple dozen of his old aunts sitting around a roaster pan of that tuna-noodle-peas-with-cream-of-mushroom-soup-and-crispy-crushed-potato-chips-baked-onto-the-top-of-it casserole and some green type of Jell-O, since leftover tuna's a no-no. It gives me warm fuzzies. For this reason I go back and retrieve that #10 can of Pocahontas sweet peas; they're not mere coincidence. He's getting a king-size bottle of queen olives, a shoebox tin of black pepper, a gallon plastic jar each of Continental Food Service Thousand Island, French, Tartar, and All-Purpose Supreme Sauce . . . he laughs out loud when he sees my face, puts back the plastic, except the Supreme Sauce. I grab the Campbell's Soup family-size cans and the Super Size Lay's potato chips, no one can eat just one, but anyway I look just to see what he thinks of it. He nods in a formal way and ritually places two institutional jugs of Tabasco sauce on the final tier of selections, then the giant stuff is over with and we turn the corner into Aisle Two.

It has peanut butter, jelly, pickles, and other things in jars. We pick up several different normal everyday items as a couple, anyone can see this. Halfway up Aisle Two is the gourmet. KISS-FM, the Beautiful Music station, is piped into the store. I never noticed this before. "Cara Mia," he says to me, reading the marinated artichoke hearts, an endearment. He offers the pickled cocktail mushrooms, pearly onions, okra. His shows me his fiery eyes with the marinated asparagus. Such a cute sweet primitive way to tickle and finesse me, pickled tiny corncobs. I want to get home right away. First, though, we must contemplate each passage. We're at the pasta now, I feel strong again, invincible . . . we look at each other but don't say a word, we don't have much use for words, since he's Indian. So we walk in the beautiful Muzak through the maze of our thoughts, which we're sharing.

It has a dreamy feel. As we walk through the aisles of the maze I can feel it. Someone bland who's not Richard Harris is singing "MacArthur Park" in the produce, the bakery. We wish him luck, as he has no passion. We silently agree on some family-paks of pork chops and mutual household cleansers. Deli, dairy, place by place we observe these homey rituals. "Here, baby, you get the good cheese when you're with me," he says at the five-pound blocks on the top shelf, handing over the 100% Natural Swiss and Cheddar like prizes. But as a timeless gesture he throws in the Bongard's processed American commodity food-program style, "for tradition." He looks stoic, dependable when he says that.

When we go by the see-through bins of candy, a colorful chaos, I know that if there were some kids with us he'd let them risk a cavity. I know that wherever we go he'll be the one to bounce them on his knee, throw them balls, give them presents, even wipe their noses. There are times when everyone wants to look the other way . . . the bright candy shapes leap at me like a crowd or revelation. My ex never wanted any children, and anyway I bet his sperm count was too low. Too lowdown and stingy. Everything had to be just so in our domicile, nothing messy, or his weak puny mind would just snap. He was dangerous. Now I'm safe. Now I'm almost to the check-out, home free. On either side of it, like the gates to a wishful sexy paradise, the shiny metallic explosive floral covers of bodice-ripper romances form a wall of entwined lovers. Racy variations on dark dashing native man nuzzling some transplanted lily, vicarious pleasures, but I am going to get the real thing.

Then he stops and tests the air, looks around himself at the molecules. I look back at him, my heart is stopped and stabbed. I stand at the checkout trying to throw him a rope with my eyes. He studies the beams of the ceiling, takes a glance out the door. Straight beyond it our getaway car is plainly and desperately visible, I only wish him happiness—won't he know this? A space of strange quiet forms somehow around him, as if there were no clatter of a hundred carts, groceries thudding, voices writhing through every human contortion, squalling babies. He has this uncanny ability. And after a moment, a century, he explains by his posture, just listen to that Muzak.

I believe it is Judy Collins singing "Send in the Clowns." I believe it is her voice that is unnervingly clear and pure with sharp instruments. I mean to say, the delicious agony of these instrumentals . . . just . . . is. I never did feel this song before. It feels so sweet, sad, implicit, the whole store should be bashful, embarrassed, subdued. But when he turns away he has this secret sort-of-a-smile. His eyes have this impenetrable glaze. They're like . . . frozen. I see this.

But I know it's only some mysterious Indian thing, once again. Some secret Indian humor. Which I am going to catch onto, real soon: everything will work out.

This is what I know. In my heart.

And believe.

And the exquisite tendril of song comes weaving all about and between us, joining us in a way that's fervent, yet calming, that I wonder, what has become of Judy Collins, the whales? and the sea . . . and my love walks excruciatingly this way, then that way, sniffing out last-minute traps—tables of candy bars, batteries, supermarket strategy for things you suddenly just can't live without. He's an oddly graceful man, moving along like ballet. His joke how he's conscious of me listening, and waiting—of course! Flowers. How could I doubt? He turns toward me with today's special bouquet and holds it out in a deeply meaningful way. I flow toward him, slow motion, four steps I'll recall my whole life.

Finally we head up to the checkout and approach it like a small essential ceremony, so happy. We stand reverently together through the total and then we bag it up and box it up and we put it in our cart and then the ceremony is over and we float blissfully up to the sensitive red carpet and the doors fly wide open for us, like magic.

"You shouldn't think so much," said her boyfriend. "It does something to your face." Y made no reply except to rearrange herself accordingly with a suitably dopey sexy smirk, glancing at the window of the downtown record store that reflected this: they looked like two 1970s rock stars, which was all she should aspire to. Smoke dope/drink wine/make love with him, Oh Wow. An older man of nineteen who initiated her into all these new nonideas. If only she'd known. Y was always seeing thoughts all over the place, no matter where she looked or how often she looked away from them, they'd be there. Gosh, he knew all the right people, had all the good stuff. A rich boy. He secretly would love her. "You fox," he said, never guessing just how sly and clever. Y put her hands in the pockets of her jeans, slouching carefully as if she were thinking about nothing, like your little-cute-sweetpink-bubblegum-centerfold-partygirl was supposed to do, constructing herself in a more and more luscious dumb appealing pose than that. Sometimes a thought would come along and scare her clean out of her mind. It would chase her up and down the streets of small towns and big cities and even into the scenery: a jungle of revenge. Later on, she would chase the very same thought down and have her way with it whether or not it wanted to, and after that devour it. Her boyfriend had been "found dead of an apparent overdose." (He never knew the line he crossed, a narcissistic injury that turned her heart to ice.) Y met many men and even some women who liked that sort of game, who one by one went missing. And even, and especially, her face, with its ferocious inquisition, they were all seduced by and strangely neuronically attracted to the calm, quick, yellow eyes of a predator, but nobody ever really knew Y.

Since you ask, what I was doing was fleeing, even before it happened. What I craved was to flee down every road, up every rise in every neck of the woods, the keen inclination and decline. How I loved the sweet curves at ninety per, the centrifugal force, the moon riding my shoulder on the gleam of a lake and the soft black nightness swallowing the urge I'd become. Arrest me? I'm a caucasian, a librarian. I could flee all night long as if consumed, not *consuming*, in the pursuit and avoidance of my initial, chronic, acute, and terminal love. It drove me far beyond alleged checkpoints of existentialist reality, flouting all boundaries, groping the ghosty white trees and their superstitious depths with my lights. Irrational aboriginal beliefs, nothing there for all your dark rumors and inscrutable dread. Only a deer I'd flush out, an owl. God, when he spoke to me, never mentioned his plan though I always felt satisfied with the explanation that the crown of creation was Man. The spirits of animals never troubled me when I lay down in my bed in the government quarters to dream. It was that girl, how she leaped away, running, elusive as wind. Even asleep, I could never get her to touch me. Instead, the hideous fact of my loneness compelled me. At first I could go to work, not dreaming, until the day I could never wake up. I was performing some evident function, but even as I spoke to visiting scholars with the help of visual aids I sensed that something had followed. Thus it was I began my long wrestle. Softer than cobwebs it was, and enveloping, causing me to somehow adhere to beliefs. That waking was the wayward delusion and error, that the thing at least would not itch. More silky I would say, seductive, like satin sheets to lovers perhaps. My foe had no form or substance and was remarkably resistant to even chance sudden words of description. Sleep. I chose to call it sleep. Every blaze of sunrise I hurtled into was victory, a glorious burst of sanguinary light. Just before the tenth grade, her doe eyes had come out of a book and unzipped me. So of course I had to try in different ways to contain the thing, hoping that no one would notice. I had already given numerous other things up for Lent. Yet I could not bring myself to Confession, save for rubbing against some girls between the bookshelves while reaching to fetch them their tomes. Therefore, on this particular evening I feared to hear His voice in the radio static or under the soda-pop-top, and listened to local Indians on their old-time memory show. Admittedly I was guzzling down the road, peering at their tribal houses and romantic lives. Somewhere, somewhere, in some yard I might see her, jumping a rope or whirling beneath the swift spiral rush of her hair. Her dizzying feet placed just so as she swung her small sister or brother, the fringe of her jacket, her skirt. The yellow squares winked on as they gathered for supper, the blue glow of TV, and then one by one winked back out. The peepshow was over, the darkness unfurled. The deep psychological night then took place. Meanwhile, two old women warbled in their lingo to apparent dismay, a rising melodious river. When their words flowed back into English they warned the public not to dance or to drink or to swear, to atone for all sins and pray the Rosary and make the Easter Duty. *Ah Maywee,* don't run about at night for the Rugaroo will surely catch up with you, they concurred. It would be like a great black dog with burning red eyes, and no one could hope to outrun it. Yet the old man who went out to play cards way past midnight was here to tell the tale. Years ago, he claimed, it had run alongside his wagon, silently pacing his horses. The words as usual flowed back into French-Indian midstream, before I could grasp the ending. In any case I keep this big gun beside me to resolve ambiguous upshots. And my headlights were the only glowing eyes in the woods, sweeping once more through the tall bony trees with their superstitious depths. No. I did not. Mention. Suspicious deaths. For a time new memory traces failed to form. You might call it a blackout. Then the sky was aglow through the bare white branches, turning the dirty snow pink with purple-blue shadows and the heart of lightness ascended. Racing again toward daybreak, joyous salvation, I glanced very quick to the side. Only a scrap of trash blown up by the wind, a plastic grocery bag or newspaper. These roadside woods well rid of wild creatures and catching the comforting detritus. I had read of the large carnivores and herds once numerous here, grizzly bears and dire howling wolves and vicious bloodthirsty wolverines, skulking lions and lynx and unconverted Indians. Moose and elk and bison and all the furbearing beavers. Also I keep this dictionary to translate their odd words as they occur and transform: l'animal, plural, *lee zanimoo*. The road snaked out before me with dull scraps of movement creeping along the periphery. My eyes were on the red heart of fire in the east that I strove for, scorning the trifling rubbish. A deep ecological sight then took place.

Weather-beaten cardboard, loping persistently in the side view, distracted me to attention. It reared up in a sudden threatening attitude the size of a bear or refrigerator. They were chasing me, I realized with freak seismic tremors. In the rearview mirror a vengeful herd of debris took up the road, to the sides they leaped at the vehicle, everywhere the maddened scraps took form with the wind and multiplied, their growth only accelerating when I stepped on the gas. Zanimoooooooooooooooozanimoooooooo they all howled as one; it came freezing through the cracks of my vehicle and seized me. 2, 4, 5-polymerizedneoprenepolyiso-butylepantherines, ooooooooooooooominous-bouncing polybutadinestyrenecopolymer puffrabbit, 2, 4, D-fiendish-playful-rolypoly-terepthalicesterployamide-otters, horrible polyethylene wolverine, no end of indestructible plastic and elastomer creation. A Wonder Bread bag writhed from the snirt in the shape of a weasel, some paper-sack raptor, an eagle or hawk, swooped to swerve me. The faster I went the more bits I passed and each bit that I passed raised up from the ditch or a snag of the brush and joined the conglomerate intention. Pinkmink of fiberglass housefur, the huge beasts of rust—numerous compounds blew out of the earth just as winged polyvinylpredators plunged from the sky dropping garbage. Beer cans and liquor bottles smashed through my windows—you yourself call them evidence. They were all over me running and flying and crawling and then a large and strigiform tabloid—it resembled an owl with the glittering false eyes and breasts of an aging celebrity—plummeted garishly into my windshield, obliterating my vision and forcing me out of control. There was a brief inexplicable glimpse of biocide drums. I suppose then I slid finally into the void, but the officers recovered me, and that is all in the matter I recall.

Item, POLICE REPORT:

White man found in landfill, DWI. Turned over to county authorities and questioned in recent killings of yard dogs, prowling. Name withheld pending additional charges.

Mekinaak Miniss Tribal News

COLOPHON

Night Train was designed at Coffee House Press,
in the historic warehouse district of downtown Minneapolis.
The type is set in Spectrum.

FUNDER ACKNOWLEDGMENTS

Coffee House Press is an independent nonprofit literary publisher. Our books are made possible through the generous support of grants and gifts from many foundations, corporate giving programs, individuals, and through state and federal support. Publication of this book was made possible, in part, through special project support from the Jerome Foundation. Coffee House Press receives general operating support from the Minnesota State Arts Board, through an appropriation by the Minnesota State Legislature and from the National Endowment for the Arts, and major general operating support from the McKnight Foundation, and from Target. Coffee House also receives support from: an anonymous donor; the Elmer and Eleanor Andersen Foundation; the Buuck Family Foundation; the Patrick and Aimee Butler Family Foundation; Stephen and Isabel Keating; Kathryn and Dean Koutsky; Tom Rosen; Stu Wilson and Melissa Barker; the Lenfesty Family Foundation; Rebecca Rand; the law firm of Schwegman, Lundberg, Woessner & Kluth, P.A.; the James R. Thorpe Foundation; the Woessner Freeman Family Foundation; the Wood-Rill Foundation; and many other generous individual donors.

This activity is made possible in part by a grant from the Minnesota State Arts Board, through an appropriation by the Minnesota State Legislature and a grant from the National Endowment for the Arts.

 MINNESOTA STATE ARTS BOARD

 TARGET.

To you and our many readers across the country,
we send our thanks for your continuing support.

Good books are brewing at coffeehousepress.org